The Sword of
Destiny

Midnight at Moonglows
Book II

Happy Reading !!

K. C. Sherwood

K. C. Sherwood

abbott press®
A DIVISION OF WRITER'S DIGEST

Abbott Press books may be ordered through booksellers or by contacting:

Abbott Press
1663 Liberty Drive
Bloomington, IN 47403
www.abbottpress.com
Phone: 1-866-697-5310

Because of the dynamic nature of the Internet, any web addresses or links contained in this book may have changed since publication and may no longer be valid. The views expressed in this work are solely those of the author and do not necessarily reflect the views of the publisher, and the publisher hereby disclaims any responsibility for them.

Any people depicted in stock imagery provided by Thinkstock are models, and such images are being used for illustrative purposes only. Certain stock imagery © Thinkstock.

ISBN: 978-1-4582-1449-2 (sc)
ISBN: 978-1-4582-1450-8 (hc)
ISBN: 978-1-4582-1451-5 (e)

Library of Congress Control Number: 2014903149

Printed in the United States of America.

Abbott Press rev. date: 03/05/2014

For my parents: Thank you for your ever-loving support and for always believing in me.

CONTENTS

Chapter 1
THE LITTLE BLACK BOOK

Casey and Uncle Walt exchanged nervous glances as they dug their heels into their horses and took off at a fast gallop toward Mr. Appleby's ranch. Now they had two reasons to worry. If this had been one of their normal trips, Mr. Appleby would've been bringing horses to them, but this time they had to pinch a couple from a nearby corral, and everyone knows what happened to horse thieves in 1880 Arizona (at least the ones who were caught, anyway). What had Casey Parker even more nervous, however, was the little black book she had stashed in the saddlebag. As it turned out, Great Uncle Walter knew as little about it as she did.

After Casey had found it underneath a shelf in the back of the bookshop, she brought it straight to Uncle Walter. They had both stared in bewilderment as they turned to the section of the book that had Thomas Appleby's name listed next to it in the table of contents. His entire life was outlined in the chapter, from birth through his years as owner of the bookshop. It ended with where he was now, retired into his favorite Old West novel. Uncle Walt's life was there too, in the next chapter, at least up until a few months ago. The last line of text read, "Walter Parker takes over Moonglow's Bookshop: June 6, 2010." Following that were many blank pages. Casey's chapter apparently didn't exist yet; her name was listed in the table of contents with blank page numbers next to it.

They had decided on a trip to see Mr. Appleby as soon as possible in the hopes that he knew something about this strange book. As they sped across the Great Plains on their steeds, the faint whistle of an old black locomotive reached Casey's ears. She involuntarily looked back over her shoulder to make sure that they weren't being pursued. The only thing visible as far as the eye could see was the line of pink and orange rock formations that stretched across the horizon. Casey brushed off the paranoia and tried to focus her attention in front of her.

Her mind kept racing through all the events of last summer, searching for some clue as to what this could mean. The summer between sixth grade and junior high was unlike any that she had ever experienced. Her Uncle Walter introduced her to a magical bookshop. The mere fact that one even exists—where it's possible to leap into a book, befriend the characters, and have adventures—is astonishing in itself. So should it be surprising that she had found a book hidden under a shelf in the bookshop with their names listed in it?

When they reached Mr. Appleby's ranch, they quickly tied up their horses. Casey pulled the book out of the saddlebag and rushed to the front door, pounding on it furiously. She could hear footsteps inside, the old man's cowboy boots clicking swiftly across the wooden floor. Mr. Appleby flung the door open.

"What the heck is going on out here?" His expression instantly changed from annoyance to concern as he observed Casey and Walter standing on his front porch, staring at him nervously. "Casey, Walter! What are you two doing here? Come in, come in."

Casey and Walter followed him inside, and the three sat down at the little wooden kitchen table.

"Can I offer you two a drink?"

"No time for that, Mr. Appleby," Casey said. "You've got to see this book I found. Please tell me you know something about it. Please tell me what this means!"

"Hold on there, Casey. Let's just slow down a second and relax." Uncle Walt ran a hand through his silvery-brown, wind-blown hair and turned to Mr. Appleby. "Yes, Tom, thank you. We would love some water. Sorry to come barging in on you unannounced like this. But I have to say, I am somewhat concerned myself about this book that Casey found."

Mr. Appleby placed two glasses of water in front of them and picked up the book from the table.

"Let's see what we've got here." He examined it closely, running his fingers over the silver letters on the cover that read *Moonglow*. Then he undid the buckle and opened it to the first page.

Casey jumped up from her chair and pointed to the top of the page. "See what it says up here? And we found another rhyme at the very back. And the lettering is different between the two. It looks like two different people wrote them."

At the top of the first page it read:

Destiny calls the chosen ones into the book of their heart's delight.
Choose your book wisely, for that's where you'll be,
Until the end of time, as you will see.

Mr. Appleby then flipped to the very back of the book and continued to read:

Through the doors, into the light,
Back and forth, into the night,
From book to book and place to place,
Through hidden doors you may face
An awful sight, an awful fright,
But to the source with all your might,
Take the key and prepare to fight,
For only then, will you see
The magic will finally set you free.

"It looks like the book is filled with chapters about the lives of all the previous owners of the bookshop," Uncle Walt said. "Or at least that's what I'm assuming because your life is in there and so is mine up until I took over the bookshop. Casey's name is in the table of contents, but her chapter is blank. I guess she's next in line. I never knew any of the other owners before you, Tom, so I don't recognize the other names."

Uncle Walt remained quiet for a minute, giving him time to skim through the book. When he finally looked up, Mr. Appleby eyed the two of them silently, an uneasy expression spreading across his face.

Casey snapped her fingers. "Mr. Appleby, please say something. This is torture!"

He gently placed the book on the table. "I've seen this book once before when I was very young. I had completely forgotten about it until now. The man who owned the shop before me, Furvus Underwood, was holding it when I came in one night to go on an adventure. I was probably only eight or nine years old at the time. I remember him holding up this book and saying that it was my destiny. I never saw it again after that. Where did you find it, Casey?"

"It was shoved way underneath the bottom shelf in the back of the store. It was so covered in dust that I don't know how I could have seen the silver buckle shining out from underneath the shelf. It seems almost impossible. It's like it was calling to me or something."

Uncle Walt picked it up and turned it over and over in his hands. "What happened to Furvus Underwood? How did the book end up there? And what did he mean by your *destiny*?"

Casey put her elbows on the table and rested her chin in her hands. "Yeah, that's a little scary, not to mention those rhymes. What does it all mean?"

Mr. Appleby slowly lowered himself onto one of the empty chairs and placed his palms flat on the table. "Well, I'm sorry that I don't have a lot of answers for you, but I'll tell you what I do know.

"It would have been, let's see, 1954 maybe. It was winter, I remember, because the air was frigid and bit at my cheeks as I made my way to Moonglow's. I snuck out of my house because, as you know, the magic of the bookshop only works at night when the moonlight is shining in. My mother would certainly not let her nine-year-old out by himself at night. Sneaking out was worth it though. Leaping into books was a dream come true. I ran through the rules in my mind: the books must stay in the shop at night, I must not forget my key, and I must be out by midnight or I'll be stuck in the book forever. I double-checked my pocket for the key. It was there. I had never forgotten my key. It was the most important possession I'd ever owned. Not only does it get you into the bookshop, but back through the door into the real world as well. Big responsibility for a little kid.

"My face burned with the cold, but I paid it no mind because I couldn't wait to leap into my next book—a cowboys and Indians saga, of course. As a matter of fact, it was this very book that we're in now. I jogged the rest of the way there, watching my breath emanate in little puffs of white steam. In no time at all, I could see the musty little shop in the distance. A chill of excitement ran through me as the wooden sign that hangs over the door came into view and then the moon half covered in clouds on the front window. I pushed the door open and found Mr. Underwood waiting for me. The man was a bit odd and seemed to always have a shadowy aura surrounding him. I thought I could almost see it—an outline of charcoal gray hovering just around the edges of the man's body. He stood near the counter with a black book in his hand and moved toward me as soon as I came in. 'Thomas, my boy!' he said. 'How nice to see you!' He put his arm around my shoulder and led me to one of the chairs in the shop. 'Sit down. I've something to show you,' he said.

"His hair and eyes were both dark as night, and he bent down on one knee to level himself with me. I sat quietly, feeling hypnotized by his dark eyes. Underwood held up the book in front of me, pointing at the title. 'This, my dear boy, is your destiny,' he said. 'Your life will be in this book. Your entire life, before and after, for all eternity. Make sure you choose wisely when the time comes.'

"I was bewildered. The man wasn't making any sense. 'Before and after what?' I asked.

"Then he said, 'Don't worry about it now, boy. Too much to explain to such young ears. I'll tell you everything in good time. Just remember this book.'

"He tapped it twice with his finger, and then he rose to put it in a drawer behind the counter. He said, 'Go on now. Get to your adventure. Don't just sit there staring at me like that.'

"He didn't have to tell me twice. I popped up out of my chair and rushed over to the book I wanted. I read the first few words aloud and immediately felt the wind begin to blow through the shop and swirl all around me. Then everything went black. In a matter of seconds, I was off playing cowboys and Indians. I never saw that book again. I ended up taking over the bookshop a few weeks after I graduated from high school because Mr. Underwood had apparently died in a house fire. His remains were never found. He was a strange one; that he was. He didn't have any friends in town, and people generally avoided him, except me. I was so gung-ho over my adventures that I didn't care. But there was definitely something dark about him."

When Mr. Appleby finished, they sat in silence, trying to process the information and come up with some sort of clue. Casey took the book and flipped through the Underwood chapter. It looked like a perfectly normal life, but it said nothing about him dying in a house fire. His chapter just ended with a date, 07/01/1963, and Mr. Appleby's chapter started on the next page.

Uncle Walt spoke first. "Okay, let's work with what we have. The first rhyme sounds like we are being called into the books forever. Like we don't have a choice. Now, we know that you chose to retire into this Western novel, Tom, but you don't know what Underwood planned to do, right?"

"No. Unfortunately he died before he had the chance to tell me anything else. I would have guessed that he would've been the type to want to spend eternity in a book, but I can't be sure."

"And what about the person who owned the shop before him? Do you know anything about him?"

"Let's see who it was." Casey opened the book to the table of contents. "Correction, Uncle Walt. Her. It was a her. And her name was Gladys Pepperdine. Does that name ring a bell, Mr. Appleby?"

"It doesn't. I'm so sorry. But you know what? If Ms. Gladys Pepperdine retired into a book, you can go ask her yourself."

"That's it!" Casey quickly flipped to the end of the Gladys Pepperdine chapter. "It says here that she retired into a novel titled *Bittersweet* and that she works in a bakery called Le Petit Gateau Heureux. Sounds French. I wonder what it means?"

"I don't know, but it looks like we've got some investigating to do." Uncle Walt rose from the table and shook Mr. Appleby's hand. "Thanks for all the info, Tom."

"No problem at all. I wish I could be of more help. Make sure you come back and let me know what you find out."

"We will," Casey said. "Hopefully Ms. Pepperdine will know what the rhymes mean. And now, we better get these horses back before anyone realizes they're gone."

Mr. Appleby walked them outside and saw them off. He waved his cowboy hat in the air as they rode away and shouted, "Good luck, you two! And be careful! When you're dealing with magic, you never know what could happen!"

Chapter 2
THE SEARCH BEGINS

The clock on the wall of Moonglow's Bookshop read half past ten. An impossibly bright October moon shone in through the storefront windows, softly illuminating the aging volumes resting silently on their shelves. A door suddenly appeared with a quiet *pop*, and through it stepped Casey and Uncle Walter.

"We definitely don't have time to go tonight," Uncle Walt said, glancing up at the clock.

"I know," Casey whispered. She always felt like she should whisper whenever she was in the bookshop at night. Everything was too still, too quiet.

"Meet you here same time tomorrow night?"

"Yes. And I'm going to take that book home with me too. I wanna check it out before we go into it."

"Good idea."

They parted ways outside the shop and headed for home. Casey gazed up at the moon while she walked along the tree–lined streets, breathing in the crisp night air. Oak, pine, and maple trees towered over her, making the moonlight shine down in patches of light that looked like pools of shimmering silver on the sidewalk in front of her. Walking in the quiet of night under the canopy of moon and stars made her feel like anything was possible. She felt strong and confident, and hope was infinite. All her worries melted down into something she could put in her pocket and crush between her fingers. Even this book she found seemed less alarming when she was walking in the moonlight. It really wasn't that big of a deal, was it? She and Uncle Walt would figure it out, and that would be that. Of course they would. But everything seems different in the moonlight, doesn't it?

It took her less than ten minutes to walk to her house, which sat at the edge of town, nestled up against the deep woods. The streets were dark and deserted, as they always were. In her tiny little town of Oak Hill, very few people ventured out after dark. First, because that's just the way small towns are, and second, because there was absolutely nothing to do. This suited Casey very well since she had to sneak out of her house whenever she went to the bookshop at night to have an adventure. The stuffed animal decoys she'd been using since she discovered the bookshop the previous summer worked like a charm. Her mother never suspected a thing. As far as she knew, Casey was sound asleep in her bed every night, and when Mrs. Parker peeked in to check on her, that's what she saw. The lumpy mound of a sleeping twelve-year-old beneath the covers.

≈

Casey awoke to the usual hustle and bustle of a typical Saturday morning in the Parker household. Her older brother, Ryan, was getting ready for work. Her dad, Joe, was heading out to rake leaves and mow the lawn. Her mother, Emma, was off to run errands and most assuredly make a side trip on the way to gossip with Mrs. Tinsley. Her older sister, Samantha, thank goodness, was still sleeping. Although things had gotten somewhat better between the two of them, they still didn't quite understand each other. Samantha was the cheerleader queen, and Casey was the bookworm. Apples and oranges, as they say.

"Good morning, Casey," her father said as she stepped into the kitchen. "Wanna help me rake? It'll be loads of fun." He winked at her.

"Sorry, Dad. I've got important business to take care of. But you have fun without me, okay?" She grinned, returned his wink, and then hurried out of the kitchen before he could say that he was serious. No time for raking leaves today; she had some reading to do.

She tied her shoulder-length blonde hair up in a ponytail and headed for the door.

Ryan was just coming down the steps as Casey passed by. "Didja have a great adventure last night?" he asked.

Ryan was the only other person in the real world, besides Uncle Walt, who knew about the magic of the bookshop. Casey had tried to get him to go on an adventure with her, but he always refused. He always had some lame excuse for why he couldn't go, but Casey could tell that he just didn't want to. She could see it in his eyes; the tiniest bit of fear was there. The magic freaked him out, plain and simple.

"Umm, yeah. It was pretty cool," she replied. She thought it best not to tell him anything about the book she had found. No need to worry him when they didn't even know what it meant yet. "Just went into the jungle to visit Kamari. Haven't seen him in a while. Ha! I see you've combed your hair for work beautifully, as usual."

"Oh, thanks for noticing, sis!" He ran his hand through the wild mass of dirty-blond hair, sticking out from his head in all directions. "You know how I like it, free and natural!"

Casey followed him out the front door and waved to him as he backed his old blue Mustang out of the driveway and sped off up the street, screeching the tires a little as he rounded the corner one block down. She turned and walked around the side of her house toward the backyard. In the daylight, the leaves on the trees were glorious shades of red, orange, and yellow.

Oktoberfest would be happening soon. This would be the first year that she wasn't going with her parents. She had made plans with her friend, Miranda, and they were going to meet up with a few others too. Things sure had changed since last year. And all for the better. She was enjoying her first year of junior high. No more bully to worry about, and she had a lot more friends surrounding her. Too bad she couldn't tell them about the bookshop. But, then again, she kind of liked having that secret for herself.

She headed for the woods behind her house, jumping in the pile of leaves that her father had raked the day before along the way. This prompted her father to issue an annoyed sigh and a "Caaseeey!" while she giggled and ran off into the woods to her favorite reading spot. When she was settled on her reading rock, which happened to be shaped like a lounge chair, she opened *Bittersweet* and began to read.

She immediately saw why Ms. Pepperdine would want to retire into this book. It charmed her right from the beginning. It was set in the hills of France, in a quiet little town called Cordes-sur-Ciel. The bakery and its owner were the main focus of the story. According to the book, the owner's name was Celeste Dufour, and the bakery, Le Petit Gateau Heureux, translated to The Happy Cupcake in English. Very special cakes and cupcakes were made in this bakery. Cakes that had magic in them. Celeste Dufour baked cakes that could let you talk to animals, allow you to hear the flowers sing, or make you run faster. A slice of her German chocolate cake would make you float through the air for a while. Every slice of her pineapple upside-down cake made you one day younger. A bite of her angel food cupcake revealed who was in love with you, and a bite of her devil's food cupcake, given to someone else, would make them fall in love with you. As a result, the town was filled with the drama of never-ending love triangles and people eating their ways to younger, but somewhat heavier selves.

As dinnertime approached, Casey closed the half-finished book and took it back to Uncle Walt.

"The book we're going into tonight is awesome, Uncle Walt!" she told him as she placed the book back on its shelf. "After we figure this thing out, I'm gonna be spending some time there for sure."

"What's so special about it?" he asked.

"You'll see!" she replied and bounded out the door to head home for dinner.

Her father was bringing in a plate of grilled chicken through the back door as Casey entered through the front.

"Just in time, Casey," he said. "Will you get the rest of the food off the grill for me?"

"Sure thing, Dad." She went out to the deck and brought in a pile of roasted corn. "We won't be able to grill too much longer, huh? It's getting chilly outside."

"Nope. Oktoberfest is coming up already. Before you know it, Halloween will be here."

Samantha and Ryan came downstairs and took their places at the table, each with a cell phone in hand, their fingers moving rapidly over the buttons.

"You two can just put those phones right out in the front room," their mother scolded. "No phones at the table. And I don't want to hear any grumbling. Your pen pals will still be there when you're done. You can insta-type them later."

"Oh my God, Mom. Seriously?" Samantha rolled her eyes and continued pushing the buttons on her phone frantically.

Ryan just laughed. "It's called texting, Mom. And sorry, I forgot. Putting phone away now." He popped up from his chair, swiped Samantha's phone right out of her hand, and tossed them on the couch.

"Hey!" Samantha stared dejectedly at her empty hands.

"Thank you, sweetheart." Their mother grinned and then turned her attention to Casey. "So, what are you going to be for Halloween this year, honey?"

"Please don't say you wanna be a princess or something," Samantha said as she helped herself to the large bowl of salad in the middle of the table.

Casey almost wished Samantha still had her phone in her hand. At least it would've kept her quiet.

"Actually, Samantha, I was going to say that I think I might be getting a little too old to dress up for Halloween. But when have I ever wanted to be a princess anyway?"

"Oh, my bad. I forgot that you're all grown up now." Samantha waved her fork in the air, dismissing the whole conversation.

"But the candy, Case. Don't forget about the candy," Ryan said. "I still go around with my friends just for the candy."

"That's true," said Casey. "It would be a waste to pass up all that free candy. Maybe I can come up with something."

Later that night, Casey's thoughts turned from Halloween costume possibilities to sweet magical cakes as she prepared her decoys for her escape. She expertly arranged some pillows and stuffed animals under the covers, flipped off the light, and quietly slipped out the door.

Uncle Walt was already there when she arrived at Moonglow's. He had *Bittersweet* open on the counter near the old black cash register. His tall frame was bent over it, leaning in close to read by the soft light of an antique lamp. The bells above the door jingled, snapping Uncle Walt out of his reading-induced trance. "Well, I see why you were so excited this afternoon," he said with a smile as Casey approached the counter. "It certainly sounds delicious."

"Doesn't it? I made sure to save room for dessert tonight."

"Here, put this on. The book is in there." Uncle Walt handed her a yellow backpack and then held out his hand. "Are you ready?"

Casey slung the backpack over her shoulders and took his hand. He read a few words aloud from the page he was on, and a breeze immediately began to swirl through the bookshop. A few seconds later, the light blinked out. Everything around them—the counter, the chairs, the bookshelves, and even the moonlight—disappeared into blackness. The breeze grew into a wind that blew hard against them, and they stood together in the darkness, waiting for it to be over. The first couple of times, Casey had been scared out of her wits, but now she was an old pro, waiting patiently for the wind and the blackness to do their thing, which usually took about thirty seconds. When the wind began to die down, Casey and Uncle Walt looked up toward the sky. They never knew if it would be night or day when they entered a book.

Rays of sunlight met their eyes as they pierced down through the darkness. The radiant light of midmorning quickly spread across the sky and enveloped them, warming their skin. They looked around to find themselves standing in a grove of trees, just off to the side of a dirt road. The door back to the real world stood behind them, closed and locked.

"Man, that sun feels good, doesn't it?" said Uncle Walt. "Especially after coming in from a cold night."

"Yes, it does. And do you smell that?" Casey stepped out to the road and looked both ways. "It smells like doughnuts, waffle cones, and funnel cake all baking together at the same time. I could just die right here. That's gotta be coming from the bakery we're looking for."

"I would say that's a safe assumption, but which way do we go?"

Hills in both directions blocked their view of anything that might be beyond them.

"That's a good question," Casey said. "We could split up."

"No. Absolutely not." Uncle Walt shook his head. "We stick together no matter what, okay?"

"Okay, okay. Sorry." Casey pointed toward something in the distance. "Look, Uncle Walt! There's smoke rising behind those hills over there. I bet it's that way!"

"Nice job, Case. Let's go."

The gravel crunched beneath their feet as they walked along the road in silence. Birds chirped sweet melodies that clung to the sugary breezes they floated upon. An eternal sweetness seemed to linger on every leaf, flower, and blade of grass in sight. It was as if the aroma of baking cakes had gotten inside of everything.

"If I lived here, I would never stop eating," Casey said.

"I know what you mean," Uncle Walt said, grabbing his stomach. "That smell is making me so hungry! It's almost as if it's luring us to the bakery."

"It *is* a magical bakery. Maybe that's how she draws in her customers."

"Well, it's certainly working on me!"

The sound of pebbles crunching and popping suddenly sprang up from behind them, too loud and quick for a human foot. They looked back to find a portly man driving a horse and carriage toward them. They stepped off the road to let the carriage pass, but the man came to a stop beside them. He peered down at them with rosy cheeks and a cheery smile.

"*Bonjour, monsieur et mademoiselle!*" he said, tipping his hat.

"Good day, sir," Uncle Walt replied.

"Oh, English! Mine is very good. You two look as though you could use a ride, no?"

"That would be wonderful," Uncle Walt said. "Thank you so much."

"Climb right up on the bench with me. Plenty of room! I would guess that you are going to Cordes-sur-Ciel, yes?"

"Yes, we are. We're looking for a bakery called Le Petit Gateau Heureux. Do you know it?"

The man let out a throaty laugh. "Do I know it? You are too funny, *monsieur.*"

After a short, bumpy ride, he dropped off Casey and Uncle Walt at the edge of town and gave them directions to the bakery. They thanked him as they climbed down and waited a moment to wave good-bye.

"Good luck, *monsieur* and *mademoiselle.* And eat carefully!" The man picked up the reins and drove off with a bellowing laugh.

Casey glanced at Uncle Walt as they waved good-bye. "I know who that guy is. According to the book, his name is Pierre Lachance, and he lost his only love to his archenemy, Louis Lebeau, because of a devil's food cupcake. Can you believe that? This place should be interesting."

Uncle Walt nodded and turned toward the town. "Shall we?"

They started down the cobblestone road in front of them. The narrow streets and walkways wound around old stone buildings and quaint little shops. They passed butchers and barbers and tailors and tiny bookshops. They passed fruit and vegetable carts with men in aprons standing behind them holding out their wares for all to admire. They passed cafes with couples sitting at tables for two, leaning in and whispering to each other while sipping their coffee. They passed a man on a bench, swaying back and forth with his eyes closed as if listening to music. A large planter full of tulips rested next to the bench. They turned a corner and found a plump woman walking two tiny dogs. She spoke to them as if she understood them, and they answered with their barks in an ongoing conversation.

"Oh, Poopsy, stop complaining! You have had quite enough treats today. You too, Coco. You had the same amount as Poopsy. No, she did not get one more than you did. Now, stop it, both of you."

Casey giggled. "Must be the Strawberry Shortcake."

"Yeah," said Uncle Walt, smiling. "I'm not entirely sure I would want to know what animals think of us."

"This is pretty cool, Uncle Walt. I can't wait to try some!"

"Me too, but let's not forget what we're here for."

"Oh, I know. I won't …"

Casey paused. A boy floating out of a shop up ahead caught her attention. He hovered in the air about two feet off the ground. The boy closed the door behind him and then leaned forward to make himself glide away.

"Do you see that? Guess we found it!"

She led the way to the bakery, which sat in a row of shops in the village square. A fountain of stone cherubs marked the center of town. They each held a bow and arrow and gazed up toward the sky, their pudgy mouths spouting columns of sparkling water into the air. Wooden benches and flowerboxes full of roses, lilies, daffodils, and tulips lined each side of the square. A few people busily made their way here and there, and others lounged on the benches in the sun.

Casey pulled open the door to Le Petit Gateau Heureux and was instantly engulfed in heavy, sweet warmth that filled every corner of the bakery. She nearly swooned in the richness of it. Uncle Walt walked in right behind her.

"Whoa, it's hot in here," he said, pulling at his collar.

The bakery was empty except for a tiny white-haired lady behind the counter, arranging cupcakes inside one of the glass cases that stretched from one wall to the other.

Casey walked past the empty tables and cleared her throat as she approached the counter. "Gladys? Gladys Pepperdine?"

The lady's head snapped up in alarm, and she gave them a hard stare.

"American? We don't have any Americans in this book." She put on a pair of tortoiseshell spectacles that hung from a delicate gold chain around her neck. "Are you two from the real world?"

"Yes, Ma'am," Uncle Walt answered. "I'm Walter Parker, current owner of Moonglow's. And this is my niece, Casey."

Tears began to well up in her eyes. "Oh my. It's been so terribly long since I've had any contact with the real world. I'm very happy to see you. I have so many questions."

"Actually, we have some for you too," said Casey. "It's why we came to find you."

"I see," she replied, wiping her hands on her apron and glancing back into the kitchen. "We can't talk here, though." She came around to the front of the counter and shouted, "I'll be right back, Celeste! I'm going to pick up some flour and sugar at the market!"

Gladys led them out of the bakery and down a side street to her home. Her little stone cottage was surrounded by brilliant wildflowers and had a water well in the yard. The stone walls of the cottage kept it cool inside, and they settled down in the living room, enjoying the respite from the heat of the bakery.

Gladys smoothed her dress and crossed her ankles as she sat in one of the armchairs. "As you know, these people don't know they are only characters in a book, so it's best to speak out of earshot. Why don't you two go first? I'm eager to know what you want to talk about."

Casey removed the book from her backpack and presented it to Ms. Pepperdine. "This is what we want to ask you about. Do you know anything about it? Or about the rhymes?"

The woman suddenly looked twice as old as she handed the book back to Casey without even looking at it. She slowly removed her glasses and began cleaning them with her apron. "You're wondering about having to go into a book forever. Correct?"

"Yes," Casey said anxiously. "Do we *have* to? Is there no choice?"

"I'm afraid you're not going to like anything I have to say. Apparently, there is no choice in the matter. Now, I don't know everything, but as I understand it, when he decides that it's your time, you have to go, whether you want to or not."

"When *who* decides?" asked Uncle Walt.

"Underwood, of course. You two really don't know anything, do you?"

They both shook their heads.

Gladys lowered her head and spoke softly, averting her eyes from them. "I had a daughter. I loved her more than anything and would have loved sharing my adventures with her, but she was a very timid child. Afraid of her own shadow, so to speak. I knew the idea of magically jumping into stories and the dangers that come with it would be far too much for her to handle. And she was never one for fantasy either. She liked hard, cold facts. Science, medicine. She went away to college to become a doctor and ended up moving across the country. There weren't very many female doctors back then. I was so proud of her. She met a nice man, another doctor at the hospital where she worked, and got married. I didn't get to see her much with her being so busy all the time, and I couldn't just leave the bookshop. But, when she told me I was going to be a grandmother, I was determined to go see her. Even if I had to close up the shop for a few weeks. I didn't care. I missed her so much, and I wasn't about to miss the birth of my grandchild. But I never got the chance."

Gladys paused for a moment, wiping the corners of her eyes.

"It was the day before I was supposed to leave. Maybe he knew that once I got out there with my daughter and grandchild, I wouldn't want to come back. I don't know. So, in walks Furvus Underwood, just before closing time. It was already dark outside. I thought he was a customer, so I asked if I could help him. He said yes and put his hand on my shoulder. I was instantly paralyzed. I could talk, but I couldn't move any other muscle in my body. I was terrified as those black eyes bore into my soul. He told me his name and asked what my favorite book was. I didn't answer. He said that it was my time and that if I didn't choose, he would choose for me. He showed me that book you have there and read the rhyme out loud. Said that it was my destiny to spend all eternity in the book of my choosing. I pleaded for my daughter, for my grandchild, for myself. He only said, 'Choose.' I whispered the word, 'Bittersweet.' And here I am. I can't imagine what my daughter must have thought, with me disappearing like that. What she must have gone through with a new baby and no mother. But that was a long time ago."

Uncle Walt went over and knelt next to her, putting his hand on top of hers. "I'm so sorry, Gladys. I'm so sorry that happened to you."

She turned to him and forced a smile. "Thank you, dear. It was very hard for me for a long time, but I've adjusted. I did always love this book, and I have made wonderful friends here who have become like my family. Celeste is one of them."

Casey fidgeted in her chair, gnawing on her thumbnail. "What are we gonna do, Uncle Walt? I've thought about the possibility of retiring into a book when I get old and thought that might be kind of cool, but I don't want to be forced into it. What about you?"

Uncle Walt got up and returned to his chair. "I haven't decided for myself yet, but I agree. I definitely don't want to be forced."

"What about this other rhyme, Ms. Pepperdine? What does it mean?"

"You can call me Gladys, dear. What does it say? He only read one rhyme to me, and I've never seen the inside of the book."

Casey read the second rhyme aloud and then related to her what Mr. Appleby had told them about Furvus Underwood.

Gladys snorted. "Died in a fire, huh? Not likely. Underwood didn't die in any fire. That had to be a cover. He's got dark magic in him. He doesn't die. He's the reason I'm here forever. He's the reason we all have no choice. He paralyzed me in the real world with the touch of his hand. I don't know what that rhyme means, but that last line says that the magic will finally set you free. It sounds to me like maybe there's a way."

"How about the person who had the shop before you?" asked Uncle Walt. "Did they ever tell you anything?"

"No. Henry Mellows didn't have any family left, so he wanted to go in. He couldn't wait. I guess that must be why Underwood never bothered with him. I'm sure he would've told me if he knew anything. We were very close. He was like a father to me, but you could give it a shot. Look him up, ask him if he knows anything, and tell him I said hi."

"Thank you so much, Gladys," said Uncle Walt. "We really appreciate it."

"You're welcome. Now, I've got to swing by the market, but you two should stop by the bakery and have a little fun," Gladys said with a grin. "Here, take a few francs."

"Thank you!" said Casey, slinging her backpack over her shoulders and pocketing the money. "I've been dying to try some."

Casey and Uncle Walt headed back to the bakery. Casey hurried him along, walking quickly with the anticipation of eating magical cakes and a bit of renewed hope about their situation. As bad as it felt to confirm her suspicion that they had no choice but to retire into a book forever, as least they were getting somewhere in figuring this whole thing out. Everything was pointing to Furvus Underwood as being the root of the problem, but exactly how powerful was he? Did he make up all the rules, or was he just manipulating them? Was he the source of the magic of the bookshop, or did it come from the moon as Uncle Walt had said? Casey found it hard to believe that someone as evil as Furvus Underwood, who played with dark magic, could be the reason that the magical bookshop existed. The magic of the shop felt too inherently good to come from something like that. No, he had to be twisting it somehow. Plus, the magic didn't work on rainy nights. The moonlight had to be shining into the shop for it to work.

Maybe there *was* a way. The second rhyme mentioned something about having to fight and being set free. But fight what? Or whom? If it was Underwood they were meant to fight, how would they find him? So many questions were still unanswered, but Casey was determined to find the way. She refused to let herself or Uncle Walt be forced into living in a book forever. And who knows, if she could destroy this dark magic, maybe Gladys could be set free. But she didn't want to get ahead of herself just yet. She tried to put all that aside for the moment because she had some magical cakes to eat first.

≈

This time, when they entered the bakery, a tall, slender blonde woman stood behind the counter. Her pale blue dress matched her pale blue eyes perfectly. The corners of her pink lips upturned ever so slightly in a sly grin. No question that this was Celeste Dufour. She fit the description in *Bittersweet* to a tee.

"*Bonjour, bienvenue pour Le Petit Gateau Heureux,*" she said, her voice almost as soft as her cakes.

"Hello," said Casey.

"Oh. May I help you find something?" Celeste said, switching to English.

"There are just so many," Casey said, perusing the glass cases. "I have no idea. They all look delicious."

"Well, take your time. Each one has a special power, and it's written right underneath the name, in English and French. If you'd like to know, my best seller is the pineapple upside-down cake, but you don't need to be any younger, little one. Perhaps you'd like to run faster or jump very high or talk to the animals? Yes?"

"If I eat more than one at the same time, will all the spells work together?"

"Oh yes, absolutely. And how about you, *monsieur*? Anything for you?"

Uncle Walt stood back a few paces from the counter, seeming a bit unsure. "Oh, ummm, I'm just looking. I'm not very hungry."

"Come on, Uncle Walt. Get over here and pick something. I don't wanna do it alone."

Casey and Uncle Walt marveled at the display. Cakes and cupcakes of every shape, size, color, and flavor lined the cases from wall to wall. Casey's mouth watered as she scanned them, carefully considering the spell and flavor of each one. The cupcakes were piled high with fluffy frosting, and the cakes were decorated with perfectly molded edible flowers.

"There's an invisibility spell, Uncle Walt!" Casey said, pointing to a cupcake called dark chocolate delight. The frosting was sprinkled with something that looked like silver glitter. "I have to try that one!"

She chose the dark chocolate delight cupcake, a slice of strawberry shortcake, and a slice of sponge cake. Uncle Walt chose a slice of pineapple upside-down cake and a red velvet cupcake.

Casey laughed when Uncle Walt ordered. "I don't think being one day younger is going to help any. Unless you're planning on staying," she whispered, teasing him.

"Well, maybe I just happen to like pineapple upside-down cake," he said with a grin.

"Excellent choices," said Celeste as she gathered their orders and placed them on two porcelain plates. "Have fun, *monsieur* and *mademoiselle*. You won't be disappointed. *Bon appétit.*"

Casey handed Celeste the francs and sat down at one of the tables with Uncle Walt to dig in. She took turns taking a bite from each cake, knowing she would never be able to finish all three, although she wanted to because they were incredibly delicious. She ended up with chocolate and whipped cream all over her face, not bothering to wipe it off until she couldn't take another bite. She looked at Uncle Walt with her napkin poised next to her cheek.

"Do I have anything on my face?"

They both laughed.

"Wise guy," Uncle Walt said and then turned toward the window. "Do you hear that?"

"Hear what?"

"Music. Coming from outside. But it's so strange. I've never heard anything like it. Like hundreds of tiny voices harmonizing together." He turned back to Casey, only to find an empty chair before him. "Whoa! Casey?"

"What?"

"You're gone."

Casey looked down and saw the chair she was sitting on, and nothing else. She touched her stomach and then her face. She could feel herself, but there was only empty air where her body should have been.

"This stuff works quick! Come on, Uncle Walt. Let's go outside and test it out."

Uncle Walt walked slowly out the door as if in a daze and wandered over to the nearest flowerbox. He stood there hypnotized, staring at it and swaying back and forth with the music that only he could hear. Casey bounded out of bakery and got a running start toward the town square before launching herself into the air. She cleared the cherubic fountain and its spray of water easily, squealing with delight as she touched down softly on the other side. And no one saw her do it. She thought how valuable a commodity those cakes would be if she could take them into other books with her. But she knew that anything she tried to take with her into the real world would only disappear the moment she crossed the threshold of the door back into the bookshop. Last summer she had tried to take an apple back with her, and it disappeared right in her hand.

Next, she set her sights on a tall tree. She ran full speed toward it and pushed off the ground as hard as she could. She grabbed a thick branch near the top and swung her body around to straddle it. She sat for a moment to catch her breath and watched Uncle Walt stare at the flowers below. Her attention then turned to two goats entering the square. Their mouths were opening and closing, but instead of bleats, words came out. Words that Casey could understand. Their voices were still peculiarly goat-like however.

"Shall we stroll by the vegetable cart?" the brown goat said. "The man may have an apple for us today."

"I should think it's worth a try," replied the white goat. "Let's go. Oh, look. I've never seen *him* before."

The two goats strutted right over to Uncle Walt. "Is this your first time?" the white one asked. "I say, can you hear me? Do you happen to have any grain or vegetables on hand?"

Uncle Walt seemed not to notice at all and continued staring straight at the flowers in front of him.

"Oh, he can't hear you, Sebastian," the brown one said. "The flowers have him hypnotized. It's no use. It doesn't look like he has any food about him anyway. Let's move on."

"Yes, Reginald, you're quite right. Let's—"

A man suddenly thrust his head out of a window above, yelling down at the goats. "Will you two just shut up? Every day it's the same thing! Bothering everyone in town for food. You're driving me batty!" The man waved his fist at them and just as suddenly disappeared back inside the window.

"Well, I never!" said the white goat.

Casey tried to suppress her laughter, but she couldn't hold it in. A stream of giggles escaped her lips.

The two goats looked up, searching the nearby trees.

"Who is that? Show yourself at once!" the brown goat demanded.

Casey leaped down from the tree and stood next to them. "I'm so sorry. I don't know how. I guess I have to wait for the spell to wear off. I'm sorry for laughing. It's just that I've never heard animals talk before."

"Well, you should listen to us more often," the white one said. "You might learn something. Unlike that imbecile up there."

"Let me assure you that we are not all like that," Casey said. "I would love to listen to what you have to say."

"And we would love to discuss the theory of relativity with you, but right now we have more important things to attend to. By the way, you don't happen to have any carrots, do you?"

"No, I'm sorry. I don't"

"Just as I thought," said the white goat. "Come along, Reginald."

The two goats flipped up their tails and trotted off. Casey watched them go and then shook Uncle Walt's shoulder, snapping him out of his trance.

"Casey? That you?"

"Yes, it's me. See those two goats walking away over there? They were talking to you!"

"Really? What were they saying?"

"They were asking you for food. And apparently they know all about the theory of relativity."

"Huh. You don't say," Uncle Walt said, scratching his head. "I feel like I just woke up from a dream."

"Yeah, those flowers really had you hypnotized. Should probably stay away from that one, but these other spells would really come in handy in some of the other books. I jumped clear to the top of that tree and nobody saw me do it. I wish we could take some cakes with us."

Uncle Walt rubbed his eyes and shook his head. "Come on. I think I've had enough magic for one day."

As they hiked back down the dirt road outside of town, the spells began to wear off. Casey was fully visible by the time they reached the door. She demonstrated her jumping skills, while she still had them, by leaping to the top of nearby trees and shaking the branches to show Uncle Walt where she was. He praised her abilities, but he seemed anxious to get back to the real world. He already had the key in his hand.

Before they stepped over the threshold, Casey took one last breath of the sugary breezes and entered the cold dark of night back home, thinking only of the name Henry Mellows.

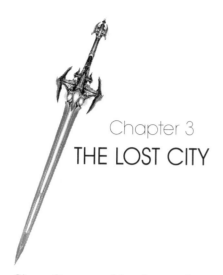

Chapter 3
THE LOST CITY

Since Casey could only go adventuring on the weekends while school was in session, she had an entire week to get through before she could meet up with Uncle Walt again to continue their investigation of the rhymes in the little black book. She made Uncle Walt promise not to go without her. Since this concerned both of them, she wanted to be there every step of the way. And in case of any danger, she argued that two was always better than one.

Uncle Walt agreed, only because he was fairly certain that they couldn't actually die while in the books; otherwise, he would never have let Casey come in the first place. Even though it had never happened to either of them, Mr. Appleby had told them that he had died once while in one of his favorite shoot-em-up Westerns. He blacked out for a few moments and then woke up again good as new. This was before he retired into a book forever, and he had said that they couldn't die because they weren't part of the story. However, once you remained in a book past midnight, you would become part of it and be subject to whatever might happen.

The only evidence Casey and Uncle Walt had that this was true took place last summer. Uncle Walt had been shot in the shoulder by a band of train robbers who were pursuing them on horseback on the way to Mr. Appleby's ranch. After they managed to lose the bandits, they stopped to check Uncle Walt's injury and found nothing but a bloodstained hole in his shirt. The wound had healed in minutes.

As long as they were out by midnight, Casey felt fairly safe investigating this mystery with Uncle Walt by her side. She just had to get through this week of school before meeting up with him again on Friday and Saturday night.

But, Oktoberfest was also coming up on Saturday, and Casey was hoping to be able to do both. As important as figuring out this mystery was, she still wanted to have some fun with her friends in the real world.

≈

The Monday lunch bell buzzed obnoxiously, and Casey headed to the cafeteria. She scanned the tables, looking for Miranda's dark hair and bright pink sweatshirt. Casey spotted her somewhere in the middle, waving her hand. The lunchroom in junior high was at least twice as big as the one in her grammar school. And instead of long rectangular tables that were assigned to each class, this one was full of round tables with open seating. People generally tended to stay with their own little group of friends and tried to get their favorite table each day. It was first-come, first-serve; when the lunch bell rang, everyone hurried as fast as they could to the cafeteria to claim their tables. The back corners were always the most wanted tables because they were the most convenient for mischief making. If your class before lunch happened to be at the opposite end of the school, you'd be stuck up front in the direct line of vision of the supervising teacher pacing back and forth, watching for spitwads and food fights. If you were lucky, one of your friends had a class that was closer and could save a table for you.

Casey didn't really care where they sat, as long as it wasn't near Sarah Templeton and her cronies. Not that Sarah ever gave her any trouble since Casey stood up to her at the beginning of the year, but Sarah was still a troublemaker, and Casey didn't need to be around that. She was there to eat and hang out with her friends, and that was it. She and Miranda and their friends usually ended up in the middle somewhere. Sarah tried to get one of the back corners—but didn't always succeed. There were a few other troublemakers besides her, and they were pretty quick at getting to the cafeteria. Casey wound her way through the tables toward Miranda, passing Sarah on the way. She quickly diverted her eyes from Casey and pretended not to see her.

"I still love that," Miranda said with a grin as Casey sat down next to her.

"Love what?"

"How Sarah totally avoids you. It's great!"

"I know. It's pretty funny, huh?"

"What's funny?" asked Richard, a slim, brown-haired boy with glasses. He took his seat, followed by Nick and Abby, who threw their backpacks down and filled the rest of the table.

"Oh, you know that girl, Sarah, that gets in trouble a lot? Well, she was in our class last year and used to give us a hard time, until Casey put her in her place," Miranda said.

"Nice," said Richard.

"So, Oktoberfest is Saturday," said Miranda, looking at each of them. "I know you're going, Casey, right?"

"Umm, yeah. Definitely. Wouldn't miss it," Casey said, hoping that it would remain true.

"And what about you guys? Richard? Abby? Nick?"

They all nodded and decided on a meeting time and place before getting in line for lunch.

"What five-star gourmet meal do you think they've got for us today?" asked Casey, grabbing a tray from the stack.

"I can only imagine," replied Miranda. "Steak? Lobster? Or your choice of old, dry hamburgers with soggy tater tots or a mystery meat patty with crusty mashed potatoes is more like it."

"You know, I really thought the food in junior high was gonna be better," said Casey, scrunching up her nose at the selection of

Jell-O squares with bits of wrinkly fruit suspended inside. "But apparently I was dead wrong."

"Hey, how are you getting to Oktoberfest? Wanna car pool?"

"I'm riding with my brother. I'll ask him if we can pick you up on the way. I'm sure he won't mind. As long as you don't mind squishing into the back seat of his Mustang."

"Are you kidding? His car is awesome. And won't we look cool getting out of it when we get there. And no parents!"

"Yeah. That's definitely the best part, huh?"

They both giggled as they sat back down at their table to eat.

"Looks just scrumptious, doesn't it?" said Richard, picking at his food.

"I've really gotta start bringing my own lunch," said Abby. "Peanut butter and jelly sounds really good right about now."

"Well, let me tell you one thing," said Nick. "If you guys are gonna eat this stuff, you better eat it fast."

"Why?" they all said in unison.

"Because you're about to see a very rare phenomenon," he said, pointing toward the ceiling. "The elusive flying potato."

A loud *splat* on the back wall turned their attention in that direction. A mound of mushy mashed potatoes was slowly inching its way down the wall when a shout of "food fight!" was heard coming from one of the back corners.

"Oh no." Before Casey could duck under the table, a couple of tater tots bounced off the side of her head and a mass of mashed potatoes narrowly missed her face, just grazing the tip of her nose. The full load of it landed right smack in the center of Richard's face, completely covering his glasses. Casey tried hard not to laugh.

"Awww, come on!" Richard said angrily, removing his glasses and wiping at them with a napkin.

"You better get down here quick, Richard," said Nick from underneath the table.

Casey, Miranda, and Abby got down on their knees under the table to wait out the storm of flying foodstuffs. French fries, tater tots, mashed potatoes, and a rainbow of Jell-O squares flew through the air. Unidentified objects pelted the top of the table like hail. Teachers yelling and running in all directions could be heard beneath the shouts of dozens of students throwing and getting splattered by all kinds of food. Casey reached up around the edge of the table to grab a handful of her tater tots and squished her hand in what must have been a pile of Jell-O.

"Ewww!" She wiped her hand on her jeans and tried again, successfully bringing them down to her.

"You're not planning on throwing those, are you?" asked Miranda. "If you get caught, it'll be endless detention for sure."

"Heck, no. I'm eating them. I'm hungry!"

When the edible storm finally calmed down, they all stood up to observe the carnage. The cafeteria looked like an artist's palette, an array of colors and shapes splattered everywhere. Mounds of squishy white goop slowly slid down the walls and dripped from the ceiling. A few kids were being dragged off to the principal's office while others were cleaning off their faces and clothes as best they could and trying to comb mashed potatoes and Jell-O out of their hair.

Casey and Miranda looked at each other and shrugged.

"Just another day in junior high, I guess," Miranda said with a smile.

"Yup," said Casey, tossing her backpack over her shoulder. "Guess we better get to class. Catch ya later!"

≈

Casey's stomach grumbled as she sat at her desk in her bedroom that evening. The aroma of chicken and mushrooms crept up the stairs and wafted directly into her nostrils, making it impossible to finish the algebra equations she was working on. She held out as long as she could and then bounded down the stairs to the kitchen, abandoning her homework until after dinner.

"Mom, is dinner almost ready?" she asked hungrily. "That smells so good!"

"Just about," her mother replied. "Would you mind setting the table and then going upstairs to get your brother and sister?"

"Sure thing, Mom."

Casey set the table as fast as she could and then ran up the stairs to pound on Ryan's and Sam's doors. She yelled, "Dinner! And no phones!" before running back down and taking her place at the table to wait for everyone.

As they all dug into their food, Casey told them about the food fight.

"Wow, I'm surprised it took until October for the first food fight to happen," Ryan said. "I thought it would've happened in the first week."

"Oh man, Ryan," Casey said. "You should've seen the cafeteria. It was a disaster area. I took a few tater tots to the head before I got down under the table."

"I've seen it before, trust me. I even—"

Casey's mother and father quickly looked up at him.

"Never mind," he said with a grin. "Yes, I've seen it before."

"Do you guys have food fights in high school?" Casey asked.

"Not really," said Samantha. "It's more of a junior high thing. We're a lot more mature in high school."

Everyone looked at each other and laughed.

Samantha paused with her fork in the air. "What? What's so funny?"

"Nothing, sweetheart," said their father, still laughing. "It's just that 'mature' and 'high school' are words that shouldn't even be spoken together in the same sentence."

She let out a huff and went back to her chicken. "Whatever. I'll never understand you people."

After dinner, Samantha took her mature-self up to her room to blast her stereo and text on her phone while Ryan and their father settled on the couch to watch SportsCenter.

Casey was helping her mother clear the table when the phone rang. "I've got it!" she shouted and grabbed the receiver off the hook.

Uncle Walt was on the other end. "I'm glad you answered, Casey. I wanted to give you a heads up on where we're going Friday night."

Casey stretched the cord around the corner and lowered her voice. "Where?"

He paused. "The city of Atlantis."

"Are you serious? That's where Henry Mellows is?"

"Yup. Get ready."

"Okay. I'm kind of excited! See ya Friday."

Casey turned around to hang up the phone and found her mother dangerously close.

"What were you whispering about over there?" her mother asked. "What are you excited about?"

Did she have bat hearing or something? How did mothers do it? Casey suddenly wished she had her own phone like Ryan and Sam.

"Oh, it was just Uncle Walt. He's got a new acquisition for me. This book I've been dying to read. And he says hi."

"I should've known," her mother said with a smile. "Some things never change. I'm glad you're still my little bookworm."

"Thanks, Mom." Casey gave her a kiss on the cheek and started up the stairs to finish her homework. "But, I'm not that little anymore!"

"Oh yes you are!" her mother called after her. "You'll always be my little bookworm!"

Casey sat down to finish her algebra, but concentrating on it was even more impossible. All she could think about was Atlantis. Atlantis. The most fabled and mysterious city in the history of mankind. The greatest civilization the earth has ever known. What would the people be like? Had it ever even existed? Or was it completely made up by Plato in his ancient Greek writings? Either way, it was supposed to have been the most magnificent city ever created, and it would be real enough when Casey stepped into it on Friday night.

≈

The rest of the school week dragged on as slowly as possible with Casey's anticipation of Oktoberfest and the trip to Atlantis. The festival was the buzz all over school, and Casey and her friends chattered on all week about what rides they were going to go on and all the different kinds of fried foods they were going to eat. They took dares on who would eat the craziest things.

"I'll totally eat deep-fried frog's legs," Nick said. "I swear I will."

"Ugh! That's disgusting," exclaimed Abby. "I bet you won't. You'll chicken out at the last second."

"As long as it's a dessert, I'll eat anything," Casey said. "Deep-fried Oreos, Twinkies, Snickers. Anything. Give it to me, and I'll eat it."

"It's true. She will," said Miranda. "She's a candy freak."

"I heard they even have deep-fried butter," Richard said.

A collective "Ewww!" issued forth simultaneously from each of them.

≈

Friday night finally arrived, and Casey hurried excitedly to Moonglow's to meet Uncle Walt. After the wind died down and the sky brightened, Casey loosened her grip on the straps of the backpack containing the little black book. They found themselves standing behind a massive stone pillar just off to the side of a paved stone road.

The smell of salt water met Casey's nose. She stepped out onto the road and had to shield her eyes from the glare. In front of her, about a hundred yards away, there was a glaringly bright white city that looked to be made entirely of marble and stone. The sun gleamed off of every smooth polished surface it could find, making the entire city shine like a giant diamond in the middle of the ocean. The road that led to the city was lined on both sides with huge stone pillars, and at the entrance stood a colossal white stone statue of a man that must have been four stories high. The legs stood apart, providing the entryway to the city. The body was strong and muscular, and the face was bearded. One arm stretched out toward the sea with a trident in hand.

"Wow." Casey stood and stared. "It's glorious."

"Yes, it is," Uncle Walt said. "And this place was said to have existed over eleven thousand years ago. If it ever existed at all. Can you believe that?"

Casey nodded. "Now I can believe anything. If you had asked me a year ago, I would've said no way."

"I'm guessing that's Poseidon guarding the city over there, judging by the trident he's holding," Uncle Walt said, studying the enormous statue.

"Oh yeah, that fork-like thingy in his hand? Greek god of the sea, right?"

"That would be the one." Uncle Walt squinted and started down the road. "Wish I had brought my shades into this one. Come on. Let's go look for Henry Mellows."

"How are we gonna find him?"

"It says in his chapter that he's a scribe here. I guess we'll have to ask around."

They passed through the gateway of Poseidon's legs and entered the city. Wide avenues spread out in all directions lined with gleaming marble buildings and temples on each side. They were all open in front, supported by pillars, to let in the sunlight and salty air. Between every few buildings were lush green gardens full of flowers and trees with sparkling fountains and streams full of fat, colorful fish running through them. Life-sized statues of muscular men and shapely women could be seen everywhere, adorning the avenues, gardens, balconies, and windows. A blanket of peace lay over the city. The only sounds to be heard were the chirping of the birds, the distant ocean waves, and the soft patter of human feet and quiet voices around them. People were casually walking to and fro and stopping to greet each other along the way. Most of the men were bearded, and all of the women grew their hair extremely long, either letting it hang freely down to their knees or pinning it up behind their heads. No one seemed to be in a hurry, and everyone was dressed in the same long, flowing white robes and soft brown leather sandals. It didn't take long for someone to approach them, dressed as they were.

"Welcome, friends," a clean-shaven, dark-haired man said. His hands were clasped behind his back, and he wore a carefree smile. "I can plainly see you are from afar. But, do not fear. We welcome visitors here, as long as they are honest and their intentions are true. And assuming you are not an enemy of the gods."

"Oh, yes, of course," said Uncle Walt. "Very honest and true. And wouldn't dream of messing with the gods." He looked down at his polo shirt and jeans. "I guess we were pretty easy to pick out."

"Not to worry. We encourage new ideas and free thinking. So, tell me, what has brought you to our fine city?"

"We're looking for someone in particular. A man by the name of Henry Mellows."

The man scratched his chin. "That is quite a strange name. I've never heard of anyone with a name like that."

"He's supposed to be a scribe here," Casey said. "Can you point us in the direction of where we might find a scribe?"

"The only scribe that I know of is Xenocrates. Turn left at the second avenue ahead, and it will be the third building on your left."

They thanked him and headed off in that direction.

"By the way, Uncle Walt, what exactly *is* a scribe?" Casey asked.

"A record keeper. They were the ones entrusted with copying down important documents: books, laws, historical records, sacred texts, things like that. All by hand. Can you imagine that?"

"No way. I'm glad I live in the digital age."

As they walked, people smiled and nodded at them. A group of children sat in a circle on the grass in one of the gardens. A man in the center was giving them lessons on some subject Casey was sure was way over her head, even though the children looked to be three or four years younger than her. They had their eyes locked on their teacher in perfect silence, giving him their full attention. Casey watched in awe as she walked by. It was like seeing a minotaur. It simply didn't exist in the real world. If they could get their children to behave that well in school, then in her mind, it really was the greatest civilization ever, if it ever existed at all.

They arrived at the building they were directed to and walked up the few steps that stretched across the length of the façade. They passed through the supporting columns and entered the cool marble interior.

In the middle of the room, a man sat at a wide wooden desk piled high with all sorts of papers, scrolls, and books. He was writing something, dipping the point of a feather into a bottle of ink after every few words. He took no notice of his visitors; he was completely absorbed in his work. The rest of the room resembled the bookshop; the walls were lined from top to bottom with shelves full of books, only it was five times bigger and also had scrolls.

Casey cleared her throat, and the man looked up from his desk. "Are you Xenocrates?" she asked.

The man rose from his chair and came over to greet them. The fine lines and wrinkles on his face suggested he was in his late sixties. He had short gray hair and a closely cropped beard and mustache. His long robes swept the floor as he walked toward them.

"Yes. I am Xenocrates," he said, extending his hand. "How may I help you, my friends?"

"We are looking for a scribe named Henry Mellows," said Uncle Walt. "Do you know him?"

A strange look spread across his face. Xenocrates seemed confused and stared at Casey and Uncle Walt, looking back and forth from one to the other. Casey thought he looked as if he was trying to remember something. Then he diverted his eyes past them and stared off into the distance.

"Are you okay, sir?" Casey asked.

His words were barely more than a whisper. "I'm the only scribe here. And that name. It's so … familiar."

"You're the *only* scribe here?" asked Uncle Walt.

"Yes," said Xenocrates. He was studying them from head to toe now, seeming to suddenly take notice of their clothing. "Where did you come from?"

Casey and Uncle Walt glanced at each other. They were both thinking the same thing.

"We came through the door," said Casey. "From the real world. You're Henry Mellows, is that right?"

Xenocrates rubbed his forehead with both hands. "I'm not sure. I can't remember, but there's something there. I get these flashes sometimes, as if I've had another life somewhere, but then it's gone. Even my name, Xenocrates, means 'stranger.' It's like I don't belong here."

"This is not good." Something began to gnaw at Casey's stomach.

"I know," said Uncle Walt. "I'm thinking that the longer someone is in a book, the more they forget their real life. I'm figuring you've been here for almost a hundred years, Mr. Mellows. This is a book you're in. It's not real life. You're from a town called Oak Hill, and you ran a bookshop there called Moonglow's. It has a magical ability to allow you to enter books. Your real name is Henry Mellows, and you were very close to someone named Gladys Pepperdine."

"Gladys. Oh my ..." His eyes widened, and he put his hand over his mouth. "Yes, I remember!"

"Thank goodness." Uncle Walt ran his hand through his hair and relaxed his posture. "That would've been really bad if you weren't actually Henry Mellows. So, how did you get the name Xenocrates?"

"I gave it to myself when I decided to come here. I thought I should have a name that fit in."

"Well, you did a really good job."

"This is truly unbelievable. Almost a hundred years you say? Time is so different here. And what the world must be like! I can see by the way you're dressed that it has changed drastically. In my time, the men wore suits and top hats and the ladies, dresses. And Gladys! How I've missed her."

Casey and Uncle Walt filled him in on everything they knew. They told him about the little book and the rhymes, and about Furvus Underwood and Gladys and everything she had told them.

"Do you know anything that might help us?" asked Uncle Walt when they were finished. "I know Gladys had said that you came voluntarily, so you probably have never heard of Furvus Underwood."

"And now I'm really scared," added Casey. "Never mind, I don't want to retire into a book. I don't want to forget my life! And you, Uncle Walt, and Gladys and Mr. Appleby and whoever comes after us. We'll all forget who we are. We have to figure something out. This can't happen."

Henry shook his head. "This is certainly a lot to take in. My poor Gladys. You know, if I had known that I would forget everything, I would never have come. And no, I've never seen that book or heard of Furvus Underwood before. But ..." He turned and looked at the shelves behind him. "I've found something strange here. It makes no sense to me, but I was hoping that maybe someday its purpose would come to light. Let me see if I can find it. I'll be right back."

While he was rummaging through shelves, Casey felt a slight trembling beneath her feet. It lasted only a few seconds and then stopped. She had never felt an earthquake before, but she imagined that must be what a tremor felt like, as if a tractor-trailer just drove by your window.

She turned to Uncle Walt. "What was that?"

"I don't know."

"The gods have been unhappy lately," Henry yelled from across the room. "They do that when they're angry. Not to worry."

He returned with a scroll in his hand and motioned for them to follow him to the desk. He unrolled it and spread it out, smoothing it with his hands and placing a book on each end to hold the curls down. The page was filled with book titles, some of which Casey recognized, and underneath each title was a small map. The books were scattered randomly all over the page with lines interconnecting them, making it all look like a tangled spider's web.

"It looks to be some sort of chart," said Henry, "but I don't know why the books are placed like this. What the connections mean.

And there are two dots on each map. Maybe you two can make something of it."

Casey and Uncle Walt leaned in close to study the chart.

"Uncle Walt, look," said Casey, pointing to one of the titles. "It's *Bittersweet*. And this blue dot on the map, it lies just outside Cordes-sur-Ciel along the dirt road. I bet that represents the door."

"That would make sense," said Uncle Walt. "It's in the right place. I wonder what this red dot is on the other side of town? It looks like it's in the forest."

"And there's *Helmlock*, the medieval book I went into last summer. And *Under the Eye of Ra*, the ancient Egypt book. The blue dots are in the right place for the doors on both of those maps."

Henry pointed to a book called *Libertalia*. "This is the only one that is different from the others. In addition to the red and blue dot, it also has a black X marked on the map."

"Well, at least we've got one mystery solved," said Uncle Walt, standing up straight and stretching his back. "I think we can assume that the blue dots represent the doors. As far as the red dots and the black X go, there's only one way to find out. Go look for ourselves. Who knows, whatever we find there may be valuable to us in some way. This chart must have been made for a reason."

"Looks like we've got some work to do," said Casey. "But we're gonna need that chart. There's no way we're gonna remember everything on it. And we can't take it out with us." She tapped her foot in thought. "I wish we could make a copy."

"We can," said Uncle Walt. "There are a few sheets of paper and some pens and pencils in that yellow backpack right there on your back. We brought it in—we can take it out. So, let's get copying."

Casey took out the supplies and sat down at the desk. "Man, Uncle Walt, you're good."

Uncle Walt grinned and winked at her. "Come on. This is me we're talking about. Did you have any doubt? You know I come prepared for *everything*."

Casey involuntarily stuck her tongue out of her mouth in deep concentration as she tried to get every crisscrossed line exactly right. Uncle Walt was right; the chart must have been made for a reason. And since it must be very important, it had to be a perfect copy. Who knew what they would be getting into? She definitely didn't want to be going in with the wrong information.

"I wish you two the best of luck," said Henry. "But be very careful. I've heard of the word Libertalia before. It was a town said to have been a pirate utopia, built in the late 1600s, on an island off the east coast of Madagascar. It was supposedly overrun by pirates as more and more of them settled there. Some of the most notorious pirates ever known were said to have lived there."

"Oh boy." Uncle Walt frowned. "I guess that would make sense why that one has the X. You know what they say, X marks the spot. Now the question is, what sort of treasure is buried there?"

The floor began to rumble again, this time a little stronger and lasting a little longer. A few books and scrolls fell off the shelves here and there.

Uncle Walt glanced at Henry with a questioning look.

"I don't know," Henry said. "They usually don't happen so close together."

Uncle Walt peeked over Casey's shoulder. "You almost done there, Case?"

"Yup, I—"

Casey's words were cut off by a violent tremor. She grabbed the edges of the desk to keep everything from flying off. Uncle Walt and Henry reached for the nearest shelf to stabilize themselves. This time, dozens of books and scrolls tumbled off the shelves and scattered on the floor.

"Please don't tell me the fall of Atlantis is beginning right now," said Uncle Walt. "Come on, Case. Pack it up. Let's get out of here."

Casey quickly stashed the pens and pencils and the copy of the chart in her backpack. She slung it over her shoulders and moved toward Henry to say good-bye. The floor shook again, almost causing her to lose her balance, and this time it didn't stop. The tremor continued, increasing in strength, shaking everything off the desk, and knocking over the freestanding shelves in the room.

"What is this?" she asked nervously. "An earthquake?"

"This is no earthquake," said Uncle Walt.

"You two better go," Henry said, his voice rising. "Run! It's the gods! Run!"

Uncle Walt grabbed Casey's hand and pulled her toward the entrance. Little pieces of the marble ceiling started breaking off and falling to the floor. A small piece hit the top of Casey's head, and she felt a sting like a bee. She reached up to rub it and felt something wet. When she brought her hand back down, she saw the blood on her fingers. It didn't hurt much, there wasn't even a lump, but the marble must have been sharp.

Uncle Walt looked back and saw her fingers. "Oh my God, Casey. Are you okay?"

Casey nodded and wiped her hand on her jeans. "I'm okay. Just keep going!"

They ran down the front steps and into the street. Everything was shaking, and the sound was growing thunderous. Whole buildings were vibrating, and huge chunks of stone and marble were breaking off and crashing to the ground. The pillars that held them up were stressed and looked as though they couldn't take much more. People who were once walking around calmly and quietly were now screaming and running in all directions. Cracks formed in the street and spread quickly down each avenue.

Casey and Uncle Walt ran as fast as they could, trying to keep their balance and avoid the falling chunks of stone and the desperate people crossing their path. Statues toppled over as they passed by the gardens, and giant stone heads rolled out into the street in front of them. They couldn't hold hands any longer because the tremors were too great. Uncle Walt pushed Casey ahead and followed behind her.

They had turned the corner back onto the main avenue and had two more blocks ahead of them to the city entrance when a huge statue came crashing down onto the street between them, narrowly missing Uncle Walt. Casey heard the crash and stopped. She turned around, relieved to see that he was okay, and waited for him to catch up.

As Uncle Walt was about to climb over the wreckage, a lightning bolt struck the fallen statue and the street beneath it, opening up a wide crack that swallowed the statue into its depths. The two sides of the crack continued to widen and began to rise, throwing Uncle Walt backward and creating an impassable chasm.

Casey screamed and ran to the edge of the hole. "Uncle Walt! What're we gonna do? You have to get over here! You have to get out!" She paced back and forth along the edge, frantically looking for a way.

"It's too dangerous here right now, Casey! You have to get out!" Uncle Walt shouted. "I'll try to find another way!"

"No, Uncle Walt! I'm not going without you!"

"You have to, Casey! We can't both get stuck in here! Don't worry about me! Now, go!"

Casey stared at him as she tried to hold back tears. Once again, Uncle Walt was right. It would do no good to have them both stuck there forever. That would actually be the worst possible thing that could happen. No one would ever know what became of them. Only Ryan might suspect that they were in a book somewhere, but he wouldn't know what to do or where to look. And even if he did come looking for them, what would he be walking into? She had no choice. She had to go.

She wiped away tears and shouted, "I'll be back, Uncle Walt! I'll figure it out, and I'll be back! I'll find a way to set you free! I love you!"

A bolt of lightning hit a nearby building, and a massive piece of marble exploded on the street next to Casey. She ducked down and covered her head with her arms, protecting herself from the flying shards.

"Go, Casey. Run!" yelled Uncle Walt. "I love you too!"

She stood up and ran for the city gate, leaving Uncle Walt behind. Thunder and lightning and stone and marble crashed all around her as she ran. The city entrance was partially blocked by the fallen statue of Poseidon, and Casey had to climb over an arm to get out. As she ran down the road to the door, she looked out to sea and did a double take. Poseidon was standing out in the ocean waist deep, but it wasn't a statue—it was the real thing. He was at least twice as big as the statue, and he slammed his trident down into the water over and over again, sending tidal wave after tidal wave toward the city.

Another bright flash of lightning made Casey look up to the sky to see a similar figure above the clouds, but instead of a trident, he was holding a bolt of lightning in his hand and throwing one after another down on the city. Casey knew instantly that it was Zeus, and with powerful Greek gods such as these taking their wrath out upon the city of Atlantis, she couldn't spare one more second.

She reached the door and patted her pockets for the key. Empty. Where was it? She always kept it in her pocket. Her mind raced, trying to remember what she did with it as things continued to crash and crumble around her. She couldn't think straight. Did she even bring it in the first place? Maybe she hadn't since Uncle Walt had his key. What if he still had it with him in his pocket? A surge of panic ran through her body. This was it. This would be the end. A pillar near her rocked from side to side and began to tip in her direction. She jumped out of the way as it smashed to pieces in front of her. She pulled her backpack off her shoulders, praying that the key would be there. She unzipped the main pouch and desperately rifled through the book and papers. Nothing. She tried the small outer pouch next and saw the glint of metal as soon as she opened it. The key. She almost cried with relief. She jammed it into the lock and leapt through the door.

The quiet was instantaneous. She turned around, almost hoping to see Uncle Walt behind her, but found only darkness and silence and shelves full of books. She dropped to her knees, closed her eyes, and let the tears come.

Chapter 4
MIZ LUNA

As the clock struck midnight, Casey pulled herself together and forced herself to get up off the bookshop floor. "You'll never accomplish anything by sitting here and being a blubbering mess," she told herself. "It's all up to you now. You've got to find a way to free Uncle Walt."

She walked home slowly, turning things over and over in her mind, trying to figure out where to begin. A thousand questions wrestled each other for her attention, but now she had no one to discuss them with, unless she were to tell Ryan what happened and ask him for help. She was pretty sure she didn't want to do that because of his aversion to magic and because she didn't want to put him at risk too. She didn't even want to think about losing someone else she loved. No, she wouldn't tell him unless things got desperate. She'd give it a go on her own first. But acting normal around him and the rest of her family and friends would be almost impossible now. How was she going to act like nothing was wrong, especially with Oktoberfest happening the next day? And what was she going to do about the bookshop with no one there to run it? Put up a closed sign?

Casey decided that was the first thing she needed to take care of. Not knowing how long this was going to take to figure out, if she ever figured it out at all, she at least needed to buy herself some time and come up with a reason why the shop would be closed. She picked up her pace and hurried home to make a sign for the window. She wanted to hang it up before morning in case the very rare customer happened to come by and wonder why the shop was closed. She very quietly rooted around in the garage until she found an acceptable piece of cardboard, some very large sheets of construction paper, and a roll of packing tape. On the cardboard, in black marker and in the neatest handwriting she could manage, she wrote, "Temporarily Closed for Remodeling." Then she took the sign, the tape, and the construction paper back to Moonglow's.

After using almost the whole roll of tape, Casey locked up the shop and stepped back to examine her handiwork. *Not bad. Not bad at all*, she thought. The sign hung on the door, and the rest of the windows were blacked out by the construction paper, preventing anyone from looking inside. She figured that would buy her a good amount of time. And if her parents happened to drive by and ask her about it, she would just say that Uncle Walt was remodeling and she had no idea when he would be done. Satisfied, she trudged back home and collapsed into bed.

The clock on her bedside table read 2:00 a.m. She stared at the soft blue glow of the numbers on her clock until she fell into a deep, dreamless sleep until late next morning.

≈

A cool, crisp October breeze blew in through Casey's half-open bedroom window, swirling around her face and offsetting the warm sunshine radiating through the glass. She stirred in her sleep, feeling the warmth of the sun and the coolness of the breeze at the same time. As her awareness slowly came back to her, she basked in the comfort of her bed, not wanting to completely wake up yet. She kept her eyes closed, trying to make the moment last. She tried to keep her thoughts at bay, but they were banging too loudly, and she had to let them in.

She opened her eyes and gazed out the window at the tops of the autumn trees, watching a bright red cardinal hop back and forth from limb to limb, singing its little heart out. She envied its happiness and seemingly worry-free existence as the full force of her situation came rushing back to her. *Oktoberfest tonight*, she thought. *There's no getting out of that one.* She had promised to give Miranda a ride, and she didn't want to have to explain to anyone about why she couldn't go. What could she possibly have to do that was more important than Oktoberfest anyway, the event she'd been going on about for weeks? Even if she could come up with some lame excuse, no one would buy it. She could play sick, but she couldn't go to Moonglow's until the moon was out anyway. Why not go and try to have some fun with her friends? She knew her mother would make her be home by nine, the perfect time to fake a yawn, head off to bed, and sneak back out to Moonglow's.

With that decided, she had the next few hours to study the chart and figure out where to start. After a quick bite to eat and a long, hot shower, Casey settled back on her bed and pulled the chart and the little black book out of her backpack. She read and reread the rhymes at least a dozen times.

Destiny calls the chosen ones into the book of their heart's delight.
Choose your book wisely, for that's where you'll be,
Until the end of time, as you will see.

Through the doors, into the light,
Back and forth, into the night,
From book to book and place to place,
Through hidden doors you may face
An awful sight, an awful fright,
But to the source with all your might,
Take the key and prepare to fight,
For only then, will you see
The magic will finally set you free.

The first rhyme seemed pretty self-explanatory. It was the bookshop owner's destiny to forever retire into a book of his or her choice. Although, as Casey had learned, if you refused to go or if you refused to choose a book, one would be chosen for you—and you would be forced to go by Furvus Underwood.

The second rhyme was more intriguing. It talked about hidden doors and a key and going to "the source" to fight. A grain of hope stirred inside Casey every time she read that last line: *The magic will finally set you free.* Set free. But how? And where was this source she was supposed to go to and these hidden doors? And fight what exactly? Was this key it mentioned the same one she had, or a different one? Too many questions. But they were clues, and they were staring her right in the face.

She looked at the chart. Blue dots and red dots and one big X. She was pretty sure that blue dots equaled the doors that led to the real world, so what if the red dots equaled hidden doors? A surge of excitement ran through her as she considered the possibility. A smile crept across her face. She might have just figured out her first clue. With a growing sense of hope, she studied the chart to try to decide where to begin. If the red dots did represent hidden doors, where did the doors lead to?

Casey's eyes kept returning to *Libertalia* and the big black X. She could kill two birds with one stone in that book: see if the red dot really was a door, and find out what that X was all about. But going into a pirate utopia by herself was more than intimidating. What could she possibly defend herself with? Take a baseball bat with her? That would hardly stand a chance against the sharp blade of a sword. It was tempting to play it safe and go into one of the books where she already knew the characters. She would love to see her rebellious medieval princess friend, Merewen, or her future pharaoh of ancient Egypt friend, Amun, but that X wouldn't let her attention go. A strong instinct was nagging at her, telling her she must start there. Yes, she would do it. Her friends certainly weren't going anywhere, and she would see them again in good time. So, there it was. Right after Oktoberfest, Casey would take her chances in the city of pirates.

She folded up the chart and placed it in her backpack along with the little black book. A rumble in her stomach told her that she must have been at it for hours. She glanced at the clock on her bedside table and was surprised to see how late it was. Almost time to head out to the festival—and not a moment too soon because she was starving. Just one more thing to do before she left.

Casey went into the garage and found a small shovel that looked like it should fit fairly well into her backpack. She *was* going to investigate a black X on the map of a pirate book, and she wanted to be prepared, just in case. She was positive it was what Uncle Walt would've done. The handle would surely stick out of the top, but that wouldn't be a problem.

She went out through the side door and leaned it up against the side of the house for easy access later. Then, she went back inside to hurry Ryan up. How did he spend an hour trying to get his hair just right when it always looked like he just rolled out of bed? Casey laughed to herself and bounded up the stairs to bang on the bathroom door. She was ready for deep-fried everything.

≈

The scent of a wood-burning fire filled the air as Casey and Miranda climbed out of Ryan's Mustang. The sun had not quite set yet, but a chill already nipped at their skin. They put on their jackets and walked through the dirt parking lot toward the festival. Orange and pink covered the sky, and the top of a Ferris wheel peeked out above the trees.

As they approached the entrance to the fairgrounds, a host of smells reached their noses: roasting meat, popcorn, and warm fried dough. Thousands of tiny white lights adorned a sea of booths that sold anything and everything you could think of. Strands of white lights were strung overhead too, from booth to booth, and giant cornhusks, pumpkins, and haystacks were scattered all around.

"This is awesome," said Miranda. "It almost feels like a dream."

"Listen," said Casey. "Do you hear that music? What is it? Polka?"

"Well, this *is* Oktoberfest," said Ryan. "Hey, you guys meet me back here at eight thirty, okay? No later, I mean it, or Mom will have my hide for not having you back by nine."

"I know, Ry. I know," said Casey. "No worries. We'll be here."

"Okay, well, you guys have fun. And don't get lost. Stick together."

"Geez, Dad," Casey teased. "All right already."

"Hey, I'm just looking out for you, squirt," Ryan said, half-laughing. "I don't wanna lose you and then have my only sister be Samantha."

"Ha. I knew there was an ulterior motive in there somewhere," said Casey, punching him in the shoulder. "Don't worry. I won't leave you alone with Sam. See ya later!"

Ryan went off to find his friends, and Casey and Miranda began to drift through the crowds. Not that it was overly crowded by any means, but in small towns such as Oak Hill, any crowd is a big crowd. They made their way toward the Ferris wheel to meet up with Abby, Nick, and Richard, ogling the food and wares of each booth they passed.

"There's just so much!" exclaimed Casey. "I don't even know where to begin. I wanna eat everything!"

"I know what you mean," said Miranda. "Oh, man. Do you smell that? Is there anything better than the smell of kettle corn? I'm dying. Come on. Let's hurry up and meet the others."

Abby, Nick, and Richard were waiting for them when they reached the Ferris wheel, and Nick already had some sort of meat on a stick in his hand.

"Geez. Thanks for waiting," said Casey.

"Well, you guys were taking forever, and I'm hungry!" said Nick as he gnawed on his meat stick.

"I know. I'm just kidding," said Casey. "Come on. Let's go then!"

The five friends went off to satisfy every bit of their appetites and then some. They gorged themselves on giant turkey legs, warm sugary zeppoles, caramel apples, and ice cream. Casey downed a deep-fried Twinkie and a deep-fried Oreo, and then everyone dared Nick to eat the deep-fried frog's legs. He stared down at them uncertainly in their little paper basket, all brown and crispy.

"Dude, you said you were gonna do it," said Richard. "You went on and on about it like it was nothing. Not so brave now, huh?"

"I knew you wouldn't do it," said Abby. "I told you you'd back out at the last second."

Nick raised his hand to silence them. "Watch and see the awesomeness that is me." He picked up one of the long, gangly legs and held it in front of his face. Then, he closed his eyes and shoved half of it in his mouth, snapping it off at the joint with a loud *pop* and crunching it between his teeth before pulling the bone out of his mouth.

"Ugghh!" cried Abby. "Gross!"

Casey and Miranda looked at each other and scrunched up their noses while Richard laughed. "I can't believe you actually did it!"

Nick swallowed hard and opened his eyes. "Tastes like chicken."

Everyone laughed, and Richard and Nick high-fived each other.

Nick strutted around and said, "Oh yeah. Who's great? Oh yeah. That's me!"

With their stomachs full to the point of bursting, they decided to check out some of the souvenir booths before hitting any of the rides. The boys had their eyes on a medieval weapons booth, which Casey had noticed as well and was excited to see. She had witnessed the swords, axes, and maces in action last summer when she attended a joust in the medieval book she went into. As soon as they entered the little booth, the man inside said, "These are purely for decoration, you know. And they are very expensive."

"Yes, sir," said Richard and Nick.

"Come on, girls," said Abby. "This is boring. Let's go look at that jewelry booth across the way."

"But I like it," Casey protested.

Abby grabbed Casey's hand and pulled her out of the weapons booth. "Seriously? You want to look at swords and stuff? Come on. Let's act like ladies."

Miranda shrugged her shoulders, and Casey followed reluctantly. Even though she had shed some of her tomboyish-ness, she'd still much rather have examined those fantastic pieces of history over perusing cheap costume jewelry, but she decided to just go with the flow.

As Abby and Miranda tried on different necklaces and earrings, complimenting each other on how cute this one or that one looked, Casey wandered off to watch the polka dancers. The *oompa oompa* beat of the music drew her over to the stage like a magnet. The men were wearing lederhosen and little pointy hats, and the women wore dresses that made them look like they had just stepped out of *The Sound of Music*. She couldn't help but smile as they spun in circles around the stage, clapping their hands, stomping their feet, and slapping their legs. She stood in awe for several minutes, feeling almost dizzy when she turned away from the stage.

Night had fallen as Casey started to make her way back to her friends. She passed a few curious-looking booths, but one in particular caught her eye. It wasn't a booth at all; it was a narrow little black tent with silver stars all over it. The sign that hung over the opening read: Miz Luna: Soothsayer, Mystic of the Night. Divinations of the Moon and Stars.

Casey stopped and stared. She had the strongest urge to go in. The little tent looked so out of place between the other brightly lit booths. It had no lights on or around it and seemed as if it was in a world of its own, far away from the noise and busyness of the festival. She couldn't resist; she had to go in to see what Miz Luna was all about.

Casey took one step into the tent and stopped to let her eyes adjust. The only light inside was coming from a single candle atop a small wooden table. Two chairs were placed on either side, and a woman sat on one of them.

"Please. Come sit down," she said. Her soft voice had some sort of accent that Casey couldn't place. She had long, dark, curly hair and was dressed like a gypsy with a long flowing skirt. Huge gold hoops hung from her ears, and noisy bangles on her wrists clinked together every time she moved.

Casey sat in the empty chair. Above her, a cutout of the moon and dozens of tiny stars hung from strings from the roof of the tent, and underneath her feet was a rug with the same moon and stars theme woven into it. Casey half-expected to see a crystal ball on the table, but there was only the candle, a stack of cards, and the silence. For as thin as the tent walls were and as noisy as it was at the festival, it was eerily quiet inside. It didn't seem like it should even be possible. She had never really believed in fortunetellers, but since there was such a thing as a magical bookshop, she was trying to keep an open mind.

"How may I help you today, young lady?" Miz Luna said with a smile. Her eyes were a bright green that seemed to glow in the darkness, and something about her face seemed familiar.

"Ummm, I don't know really," Casey said. "I just had the urge to come in."

"Ah, yes. They do that." Miz Luna laughed softly.

"Who does what?"

"The celestial forces of the heavens, the moon and the stars. The same force of the moon that causes the ocean's tides. The moon is very powerful, you know. And it knows things, as do the stars. They are more than just great balls of gas. Their alignment with each other and the constellations aren't just random gatherings. They tell us things all the time. All we have to do is listen. And they brought you in here because they wanted to tell you something."

Casey began to think that maybe she *was* crazy. The moon causing a random incidence of magic was one thing, but talking to you? Telling you things? Not a chance. "So, what do the moon and stars want me to know? And how do you know what they're saying? I don't see a crystal ball or anything. Do they talk through those cards?"

Miz Luna laughed a high-pitched tinkling sort of laugh. "No, my child. No crystal ball, and these are just tarot cards. These really are random, but some people believe in them, and they are sometimes useful. All I can tell you is that I just *hear* them. I can't explain how." She held out her arms in front of her with her palms up. "Here, place your hands in mine."

Casey hesitated for a moment, but she was too curious about what the moon and stars could possibly have to tell her. She gently placed her palms on Miz Luna's and sat quietly.

Miz Luna closed her eyes. She was so still for the next several minutes that she seemed to not even breathe. Casey began to wonder if she was all right and thought maybe she should say something or move her hands and give her a poke, but then Miz Luna finally opened her eyes and took a deep breath. They both sat back in their chairs and relaxed.

Miz Luna smiled and seemed excited when she spoke. "Well, my child, you certainly know the moon, don't you?"

"What do you mean?"

"You have a connection. I felt it as soon as your hands touched mine, a sort of tingly vibration. You know the moon, and the moon certainly knows you. You come alive in the moonlight like no one else can. You go to very special places at night. Secret places. Through secret doors." Casey just stared at her with her mouth hanging slightly open. "I can see that I am correct, no?"

"Yes," Casey barely managed to whisper.

"Well, there is a very important message for you," Miz Luna continued. "You must find the Moonstone and return it to its proper place. Protection you will find in ancient sands. Your might lies within the deepest of caves in the darkest of mountains."

Casey instantly deflated. "What is a Moonstone, and where is its proper place?" She had been hoping to hear something spectacular, something life-changing, like it was her destiny to become the first female president of the United States, not something about some sort of rock that made no sense to her. This sounded like another riddle, and she had had enough riddles already. "I have no idea what that means."

"I'm sorry I can't tell you any more than that. I don't know what it means either, but let me assure you that it must be very important. Please do take it seriously."

Casey rose from her chair. "Thank you, Miz Luna. I do appreciate it. How much do I owe you?"

"Nothing, my child." Miz Luna rose from her chair as well and gently took Casey's hand in between hers. "Just promise me that you will remember that message, and do not dismiss it as nonsense. You didn't find me by chance. You were sent to me."

Casey nodded and thanked her again as she left the tent. Back out in the noise and bright lights of the festival, Casey tried to make sense of what had just happened as she walked back to find her friends. Her instinct told her to believe Miz Luna. She said things she couldn't possibly have known. Even though she hadn't come right out and said anything about a magical bookshop, the fact that she knew Casey went to visit secret places through secret doors at night was close enough. She figured she'd better keep that message in mind just in case. As she walked absentmindedly past the bumper cars, she heard her name being called.

"Casey!" yelled Miranda. "There she is, guys. Where have you been? We thought we lost you for good."

"Oh, hey, guys!" Casey said, snapping out of her thoughts. "Sorry. I wandered off to watch the polka dancers and then got distracted by a couple of booths I wanted to check out."

"Come on. Duck under the rope and get in line with us," said Richard. "We're all gonna give each other whiplash on the bumper cars."

Casey joined them in line and enjoyed herself for the rest of the evening as they hit up the bumper cars, the Ferris wheel, the swings, the fun house, and a haunted house ride that was so bad that it was good. They laughed hysterically as they made fun of the poorly painted rubber zombies and skeletons that jumped out at them.

When it was time to head back to the entrance to meet Ryan, Casey and Miranda said good-bye to their friends and walked slowly, trying to make the night last.

"I don't wanna go home yet," Miranda said. "Tonight was so fun. I don't want it to end."

"I know. Me too," said Casey. "It felt like we were far away on vacation for a few hours, and now it's back to the real world. School. Homework. Ugh."

"Yeah, but at least tomorrow is Sunday. One more day till school."

"True. Gotta look on the bright side, right?"

They were coming up on the polka stage, and Casey kept her eyes peeled for Miz Luna's tent, wanting to see it again before they left. She scanned the booths on her left, waiting to see a dark little spot containing a dark little tent. Then they were directly in front of the polka stage. Casey stopped and turned around, completely confused. She thought it was going to be on her left. Maybe she was remembering wrong, and it was actually on her right.

"What's up, Casey?" asked Miranda. "Why'd you stop?"

"Oh, there was this booth I wanted to stop at on the way out. I could've sworn it was right along here," Casey said. "Hold on, I'll be right back."

Casey quickly jogged back up the row of booths, looking on the opposite side as she ran. Nothing. She jogged back to Miranda, scanning both sides along the way, but the tent was nowhere in sight. Her pulse quickened. She was 100 percent positive that the tent should've been along that row.

"You okay?" asked Miranda. "Find what you were looking for?"

Casey shook her head, slightly out of breath. "No, but it's okay. Come on. Let's go meet Ryan."

Chapter 5
THE BAOBAB TREE

Casey slipped quietly out the front door and crept around to the side of the house. She put the shovel in her backpack and zipped it up as best she could, leaving part of the handle sticking out. She walked to Moonglow's with Miz Luna on her mind. It almost felt like a dream she'd had, but she knew it wasn't. It definitely had happened. And the fact that the tent was nowhere to be seen when they were leaving just made her want to believe more. She was going to take that message seriously and keep her eyes and ears open for anything relating to a Moonstone, whatever that was. She wrote the whole message down on the bottom of the chart so she wouldn't forget. It couldn't hurt, right? Always better to be safe than sorry.

She entered the bookshop and locked the door behind her. It was pitch black with the construction paper covering all the windows. She hated seeing the shop like this. That cozy, homey feeling was completely gone. Just knowing Uncle Walt was trapped inside one of the books made it feel so empty, so lonely, so *final*. But it wasn't final yet. Not if Casey could help it. She made her way over to one of the reading lamps and switched it on. Then she searched for *Libertalia* on the shelves. When she found it, she brought it back over to the lamp and turned to the first page. She read the first few words and waited. Nothing happened. No wind, no darkness, no nothing. The lamp beside her continued to shine, and everything remained perfectly still.

Casey became alarmed. Had the magic stopped working? She read a few more words, but still nothing happened. No, this couldn't be happening. That would mean Uncle Walt really was trapped forever, and she would never see him again. She looked around, wondering what to do, when it dawned on her. The moonlight. There had to be moonlight shining in for the magic to work, and the windows were completely covered with all that horribly depressing construction paper.

Casey breathed a huge sigh of relief and walked over to one of the side windows. She lifted the corner of the construction paper to let the moonlight shine in, opened the book again, and read a few words. The wind immediately started to swirl around the shop. Casey pulled an elastic band out of her pocket and put her hair up in a ponytail as she waited for the wind and darkness to do their thing.

She shed her jacket, set her mouth, and whispered, "Libertalia, here I come."

≈

Before Casey could even see anything, she felt the wind swirling around her turn warm and moist. The cold October chill was gone in a matter of seconds. When the sky began to lighten, she was standing in a heavily wooded area. Palm trees were mixed with other densely green trees and shrubbery, and the air smelled salty. A symphony of birdsong surrounded her. Parrots squawked happily, and dozens of other brilliantly colored tropical birds sat on branches above and chirped their sweet songs.

Casey turned around in a circle, trying to figure out which way to go. According to the map on the chart, the red dot was on the opposite side of the island, but the black X was located on the mainland of Madagascar. She would have to figure out a way to get across the water. The black X was her first priority. She had to find out what was there before possibly going through any secret doors. More dense forest surrounded her on all sides. All she could see was green, green, and more green, except for a small spot slightly off to her right. A bit of blue peeked between the trees. It had to be the ocean.

She set off through the trees, heading for the blue spot and keeping it straight in front of her as much as possible. She continually broke branches along the way, hoping it would help her find her way back to the door. This one was well hidden compared to all the other doors she had been through, but she figured she better get used to it since she was going to be searching for all kinds of hidden doors. Better start bringing something to mark trails with. Maybe a can of spray paint next time. That would definitely be better than looking for broken branches.

As the blue in front of her grew wider and the trees became less dense, Casey began to hear sounds of civilization. A multitude of voices were talking, laughing, singing, and shouting. Children giggled and screamed. A flute was being played somewhere, and dogs were barking. She could also smell meat roasting on a fire. But what she found when she finally reached the edge of the forest wasn't much of a civilization at all.

She stayed hidden in the trees for a few minutes to check out the scene first. The "town" in front of her consisted of a few muddy dirt lanes lined with wooden shacks that seemed to serve as houses. The children were running around barefoot with tattered clothes and filthy faces. The men were also dirty with scraggly beards, and many of them were missing limbs. Most of them also carried swords at their sides. *Probably the reason for the missing limbs*, Casey thought.

Some of the men were strolling about with large iron mugs in their hands, and others were playing cards at makeshift tables. Casey watched two men get into an argument over a card game. One man stood up and knocked over the table, unsheathing his sword and holding it to the other man's neck until someone else came by and broke them up.

The dogs wandering around were skinny, their ribs sticking out under their fur. They sniffed the ground, looking for any scraps of dropped food. The only woman Casey saw quickly walked from one house to another carrying a basket of bread. In a town like this, it was no wonder the women stayed inside.

Beyond the muddy lanes of houses, Casey could see a blindingly white sandy beach and the bright turquoise blue of the ocean. A few pirate ships floated offshore, looking dark and menacing with their black flags flying and cannons sticking out of their sides. They looked so out of place in the clear blue water, and the dreariness of the town was in complete contrast to the beauty of the forest and the bright white beach.

This was going to be tougher than she thought. She didn't see a friendly face anywhere, and if she was going to get to the mainland, she'd have to get there by boat. She didn't imagine any of these pirates would up and offer her a ride out of the goodness of their hearts.

"Hey, why are you hiding in these trees spying on us?" a voice said from behind Casey.

Startled, she whirled around to find a boy of about eleven or twelve staring at her. His long brown hair hung in his eyes and looked like it hadn't been washed in months. Like the other children, he was barefoot, and his clothes were ragged and dirty. His pants stopped at about mid-calf, and the material left hanging was torn. His feet were black with mud and dirt, but his face was handsome. When he brushed his hair out of his eyes, they were the color of the sea.

"Oh, I wasn't spying exactly," Casey said. "I was just trying to figure out if it was safe."

"Let me tell you something," the boy said. "This place is anything but safe."

"I was afraid of that. How did you know I was here?"

"I didn't. I was on my way back from looking for berries to eat and found you. What are you doing here anyway? You don't look like any of the kids around here. You're too clean. And this is a dangerous place for a girl to be wandering around on her own."

The boy looked at Casey uncertainly. His eyes kept flickering to the village as if he was afraid of something. He seemed as if he was either afraid of *her* or afraid of being seen with her.

Casey decided to play it safe and test the waters a little first. "I know. But there is something really important I have to do. It's kind of a matter of life and death, but I can't explain why. It's a secret dangerous mission, and I need someone to help me. Someone brave that I can trust. Do you know anyone like that?"

She hoped to spark the daring hero instinct in him, if he had one. The boy thought for a moment before answering.

He continued to stare at her, looking her up and down, like he was trying to decide if he could trust her too. Finally he said, "Well, you're in luck because there's no one braver than me around here. And no one smarter either. So, you're gonna need me if you want to stay alive and accomplish your mission. They don't take kindly to strangers around here. Even young girls like yourself. What with the crazy way you're dressed and such, they'll take you for a spy and keelhaul you in a second."

"Thank you very much," said Casey. "I do appreciate it, and I sure am lucky to have found the bravest boy on the island. I definitely don't want to be keelhauled, that's for sure." She extended her hand to him. "I'm Casey, by the way."

"I'm Tristan," said the boy, shaking her hand. "So, what's this mission we're going on?"

"I need a boat. I'm looking for something on the mainland, and I don't think those pirate ships are gonna get me there."

"I've got just what you need. I've got my own rowboat down the beach a ways. I built it myself, and I use it to go fishing. See, I told you I was smart. It'll take us about an hour to row over to the mainland. Come on. Follow me. We've got to keep you out of sight."

Tristan led Casey through the forest, around the outskirts of town, and out to the beach. They walked along the water on the soft white sand for about a quarter of a mile until they came to his little rowboat. With the ugly, dismal town out of sight, the place was like paradise. Tall, curved palm trees reached out over the sand, providing shade and swaying gently in the breeze. The water was crystal clear, and when they pushed the boat out and got in, Casey could see straight down to the bottom, even when they reached deep water. She was fascinated by the sea turtles and the colorful fish swimming beneath them. She asked Tristan if he knew what kinds of fish they were, and surprisingly, he did. He pointed out a brilliant yellow and white striped butterfly fish, a glittering rainbow fish, and a puffed up puffer.

"I keep telling you, I'm the smartest one in town," he said with a grin. "My mum taught herself how to read, and she taught me. She says that reading and writing are important and that she doesn't want me to grow up to be a pirate. She wants me to make an honest living and says I can be anything I want. I've got some books stashed at home, and I try to get as many as I can when we are away at different ports around the world."

"Wow. I'm impressed, Tristan. Okay, I believe you. You are the smartest one in town. And your mother is a very smart lady too. That's some good advice. So, what do you want to be when you grow up?"

Tristan's brows furrowed at the thought. "I'm not sure, but sometimes I've half a mind to run away when we're docked at some port somewhere. But I can't leave Mum behind."

"I see. That's very sad. But, maybe when you're old enough, you can find a way to get out of here and take your mom with you," Casey said hopefully.

Tristan seemed to brighten up a little then. "Yes, maybe so."

≈

When they reached the shore of the mainland, Casey and Tristan hopped out of the boat and dragged it up on the beach. Casey took the chart out of her backpack and studied it. Surrounding the X were three trees arranged in a triangle. The way the trees were drawn was very peculiar. She had done her best to draw them correctly when she was copying the chart. They had thick trunks and the only branches on them were at the very top. She showed Tristan the map. He seemed to know a lot about this place; maybe he could help.

He took one look at it and said, "Those are Baobab trees, and I know exactly where to find them."

This young pirate boy with his dirty, tattered clothes continued to amaze Casey at every turn. It proved just how much looks could be deceiving. She truly hoped that one day Tristan would be able to get away and become something great. She would have to read this book when everything was over to find out. She hoped he was a main character. She would be highly disappointed if he wasn't and she never found out what happened to him.

They walked off the beach and into the trees of the mainland. The forest wasn't as thick there, and after a short while, it opened up onto an expanse of the funniest-looking trees Casey had ever seen. They were tall and had enormously thick, smooth trunks that were completely bare of branches. Just like in the picture on the map, all the branches and leaves were at the very top, making it look like it was planted upside down, with its tangle of roots at the top and its leafy branches stuck down in the ground.

"What funny-looking trees," Casey said. "They're upside down."

"Yes, some people call them that," Tristan said. "The natives around here believe that their gods became angry with this tree because it was jealous of other trees, so the gods uprooted it and stuck it back in the ground upside down."

Intrigued, Casey turned to look at Tristan. "Really?"

He nodded and continued, "It's also called the Tree of Life or the Monkey Bread tree, but I like to call them Baobabs. They can be used for survival in every way. You can make clothes and shelter out of the bark. They hold water inside of them that you can drink. And you can eat the fruit that grows on them. The fruit is what they call monkey bread, and it's pretty good too."

"You never cease to amaze me, Tristan," said Casey, gazing at the grove of magnificent trees. "These trees are awesome. And somehow we have to find three of them in a triangle. It looks like there are several possibilities."

"What exactly are we looking for in the triangle?"

"I'm not sure, but I brought this," said Casey, pulling her shovel out of her backpack.

They walked slowly through the grove of trees, checking out all the spots where the Baobabs seemed to form a triangle. They started digging numerous times, but after going down a few feet and finding nothing, they gave up and moved to the next spot.

"This is impossible," said Casey, exasperated. "We could do this for days, months even, and never find anything. There are just too many trees! They all look like they're in triangles!"

Casey threw her shovel aside and sat down against the trunk of the nearest tree, wiping sweat from her brow. Tristan was a few yards away, digging through the dirt with his hands. She watched him for a few minutes and then gazed off into the distance past him. Something caught her eye on one of the trees behind him. It looked like something was carved on its trunk. She walked over to the tree, tracing her finger over the mark. A small X was carved into the bark.

"Tristan! Come here! I think this is the spot!" She turned around to the trees surrounding her. "There's another X on that tree and another on that one. And they're in the shape of a triangle! Here, bring the shovel."

Tristan started digging in the center of the triangle, furiously throwing shovelfuls of dirt over his shoulder. Three feet down, he started to tire a bit, but he refused Casey's offer to take over. He kept going, although somewhat slower than before, and after a few more feet, he hit something hard. The shovel made a loud *clunk,* and the sudden force of it vibrated up his arms.

"Ow!" exclaimed Tristan, shaking out his arms. "I think we found it." He cast the shovel aside and dug around the edges with his fingers, clearing the dirt from the sides. He pulled out a small wooden chest, no bigger than a child's jewelry box. "This is it? This is what we've been doing all this digging for?"

Casey laughed. "Sometimes great things come in small packages. Like you, for example. You didn't think we were looking for buried treasure, did you?"

"I can hope, can't I?" asked Tristan, handing the chest over to Casey. "Here, be my guest."

Casey undid the latch and lifted the lid. Inside there was an old iron key; it was similar to the one she had for the bookshop, except that the pattern of the teeth was different. Next to the key was a stone. It was a translucent milky white color and about the size of an orange. Little ruts and divots covered its surface, making it look like a tiny version of the moon itself. This had to be the Moonstone. Miz Luna was for real, and apparently she was right. Was the key for the hidden doors? There was only one way to find out. It was time to take this treasure and get out of town.

Tristan shook Casey's shoulder. "Hey. Anyone home in there?"

Casey snapped out of her thoughts. "Sorry, I was contemplating."

"What's the key for?" asked Tristan. "And what kind of rock is that?"

"I don't know yet," answered Casey, placing the chest into her backpack along with the shovel. "But I intend to find out."

Chapter 6
CAPTAIN SCABBARD

The pair made their way back to the beach and shoved off in the little rowboat again. They chatted happily and watched the sea life below until Tristan spotted two black dots on the horizon. His face grew tense as the black dots grew bigger.

"What's wrong?" asked Casey.

"Trouble," said Tristan.

Not being able to out-row them, they waited for the two pirate ships to overtake them. One sailed up on each side of the rowboat, leaving them nowhere to go. The ships towered over them, blocking out the sun with their massive hulls and tall black sails. A rope ladder tumbled down the side of one of them.

"Tristan, I'm scared," said Casey, grabbing his hand. "What do we do?"

"The only thing we *can* do," he said. "We go up. Follow me."

Tristan reached for the ladder and climbed with Casey close behind. He threw his leg over the railing when he reached the top and pulled himself up and over. Then he turned around to help Casey. They stood together in silence while a dozen or so dirty, grinning pirates surrounded them. Many of them were missing teeth, making their grins look more like grimaces, and the teeth they did have were closer to black than white. One of them was wearing an eye patch, and another was missing part of his leg from the knee down. In its place was a knobby piece of wood that clunked loudly on the deck with every step he took. Another had several long, nasty scars crisscrossing his face. They all had long, scraggly hair and beards, and some of them wore hoop earrings.

The menacing, mangy bunch gathered in a semi-circle, silently glaring at the two friends. Casey's legs felt jittery beneath her. She leaned against Tristan slightly to stabilize herself, not wanting to show any fear, and she felt him tense up to support her. She tried to wipe her face clear of any emotion as they waited to find out their fates. Would it be the sword? Walking the plank? Keelhauling? As far as she understood, keelhauling meant they would tie you to a rope and drag you back and forth underneath the ship until you drowned—while the barnacles tore the skin from your body. Walking the plank sounded like a walk in the park compared to that. Casey actually found herself praying to walk the plank. At least she could swim and attempt to save herself, that is, if there weren't any sharks down there. She began to question why she hadn't brought Ryan with her, but then she stopped herself. This was exactly why. Because then she would've been standing there with Ryan instead of Tristan, waiting to be run through with a sword or who knows what. Yes, she was sure she had made the right decision not to involve him.

Finally, there was some movement in the circle of pirates. Two of them stepped aside to make room for someone coming across the deck. A tall, solidly built man with long, curly dark hair walked slowly toward them. He was cleaner than the rest, and his pants weren't torn. His black boots shined, and he wore rings on his fingers and a thick gold chain around his neck. When he stepped through the circle of pirates, he smiled. Casey saw that he had all his teeth, yellow as they were.

"Aye, what do we have here?" he asked, eyeing each of them. "Our lad Tristan and a strange girl with strange clothes."

Casey and Tristan remained silent as he circled them.

"And what be this here?" He pulled Casey's backpack off and walked back around to face them.

"That's mine!" Casey burst out involuntarily, her face instantly turning red with anger and panic.

"Oh, I think it be mine now, little lady. And ye might want to control that temper. Ye don't want to get on my bad side already, do ye? We only just met."

Casey took a few deep breaths and tried to calm herself down.

"Aye, now that's better. Why don't ye tell me yer name, so as we can get better acquainted?"

She kept quiet and gave him her hardest stare.

"Not talking now, I see. Well, let me introduce myself. I'm Captain Scabbard, and I be in charge of this motley crew here. They're as hard a pirates as you'll ever see. And they'll do whatever I tell 'em, little girl or not. They'd run their own mum through with a sword if I told 'em so."

The pirates laughed, looking at each other and nodding. Captain Scabbard walked slowly along the line of pirates, stopping to introduce a few who seemed particularly threatening. "See him here? This be Peg Leg Pete," he said, putting a hand on the man's shoulder. "He was captured off the coast of Spain once and put in shackles. He cut off his own leg to escape and took a few of 'em down on his way out."

Peg Leg Pete grinned and said, "Miss."

Captain Scabbard took a few more steps and stopped by the man with the scarred face. "This be Cutthroat Bill. He's given out a thousand more scars than he's received. And worse. Sometimes his victims don't recover."

"Aye," said Cutthroat Bill, running a finger across his throat. Then he nodded and said, "Miss."

"Over here be Coldblood," continued Captain Scabbard. "And the one with the patch be Red Eye." Both pirates gave a half-bow. "And see that other ship over there? That be Greybeard's ship. He's twice as mean as me and hates children, so if yer thinking of jumping ship, he'll be waiting. Ye should thank yer lucky stars that I picked ye up first."

Casey looked across to the other ship and saw an ominous figure with the longest beard she'd ever seen. It reached all the way to his knees and was the color of the sky on a dark cloudy day. He watched them from the ship's giant wooden steering wheel.

Captain Scabbard knelt in front of Casey on one knee and said, "So, why don't we try this again and tell me yer name?"

"My name is Casey," she said, staring him directly in the eyes.

"And what are ye doing here, Casey?"

"I was looking for something."

"Something that might be in this bag right here?" He pulled open the zipper of the backpack, fumbling with it a little bit. "Aye, this is a strange contraption, this is. Ye must be hiding something."

He pushed the shovel aside and removed the chest. The other pirates shuffled forward a bit to get better looks. He opened it, picked up the key for a moment, and then put it back. He took out the Moonstone and examined it closely, turning it over and over in his hands. "Well, this is interesting. It looks like ye got something that might be worth a penny or two. I never seen a rock like it anywhere before. What are ye doing with these things here?"

"Nothing," said Casey, trying to sound as casual and indifferent as possible. "They're just my things, and they aren't worth anything, except to me. That's just a plain old rock I found that I wanted to add to my collection."

"I'll be the judge of that, if ye don't mind," said the captain, placing it back into the backpack. "Yer a strange child, ye are. And I don't know where ye came from. Perhaps yer bewitched. I can't have ye wandering around bewitching my men." He turned to face the pirates he had introduced before. "Take them below. And put this away while I decide what to do with her. I'll deal with you later too, Master Tristan."

Four of the pirates advanced on them. Cutthroat Bill and Red Eye each seized one of Casey's arms, and Peg Leg Pete and Coldblood grabbed Tristan.

Casey immediately started thrashing around, trying to pull free. "Let me go! Let go of me!" They ignored her and began to drag her across the deck toward a set of stairs that led below. Captain

Scabbard laughed and walked off to his captain's quarters at the head of the ship.

Tristan didn't resist at all. He let the pirates take him and tried to calm Casey down along the way. "Don't fight, Casey. Just go along with them. It'll be okay. Trust me."

Casey took one look at his face and stopped struggling. It was pointless anyway. She wasn't going to best two hulking pirates, and even if she managed to pull away, where would she go? Jump ship and be pulled aboard by Greybeard? No, thank you. She relaxed and let them lead her down into the belly of the ship. As soon as they descended below deck, Casey was hit by a wall of stifling hot, musty, foul-smelling air. It seemed like she could almost taste it, and it did not taste good. It was dark, and it took a few seconds for her eyes to adjust. Lanterns were hung from above, dimly lighting their way as they swung back and forth with the sway of the ship, briefly illuminating things as they passed.

Casey saw sleeping quarters on both sides of her; the ramshackle bunk beds were strewn with ratty blankets and dirty gray pillows. They continued on into a section of the ship with two barred cells. The pirates opened both doors and shoved Casey into one and Tristan into the other, knocking them to the ground. Then they locked both doors and turned around to leave.

"Have fun, kiddies!" said Peg Leg Pete with a laugh. "I hope the cap'n doesn't decide to keelhaul ye both!"

The other pirates laughed with him as they disappeared into the darkness. Finally left alone, Casey pushed herself up off the ground and rushed to the bars that separated her and Tristan.

"What are we gonna do?" she whispered desperately. "This is awful! I can't stay here. And I need my things!"

"Don't worry," Tristan said calmly. "I'll think of something. And I'll get your things back. I know where they'll put them."

"But, what if they decide to keelhaul us?"

"Most likely not. Captain Scabbard is full of hot air. It's the other pirates you've got to watch out for. And he's right about Greybeard.

We're lucky we didn't get picked up by him." Tristan started looking around his cell while he spoke. "I don't think the captain would keelhaul a little girl or run her through. He's probably just trying to scare you. Maybe he'll have you walk the plank though. He also might be afraid that you're a witch. There's no telling what he'll do then."

"Great. You're making me feel so much better."

"Sorry. I'll figure something out."

Casey inspected her cell too. The floor was wood, but there was a thin layer of hay over it, making it slightly softer to sit on. One lantern hung outside the cells, just out of reach, and there was a small porthole in both that let in some light and fresh air. Casey rushed over when she saw it and stuck her face up to it. It wasn't big enough to fit her head through, but it allowed her to breathe in huge gulps of fresh air and feel the cool breeze on her face. "That feels so good!" she exclaimed. "And it smells so good! I'm just gonna stay right here."

Tristan laughed and said, "I know. These pirate ships smell pretty foul. Just look at the men who live on them for months at a time without bathing. But you actually get used to it after a while."

"I don't know about that," said Casey, turning back to face her cell. She scanned it again and noticed a large pot in a dark corner. "What's that pot for?"

Tristan laughed again. "That's your bathroom."

"Oh … my … God."

Not being able to find a way out, Casey and Tristan sat down on the hay and waited. Casey sat close to the porthole so she could feel the outside air and see the deep blue of the sky. The ship creaked as it rocked gently on the waves, almost lulling her to sleep, until a shout from above drew her attention back.

"What was that?" she asked.

"It sounded like the call to weigh anchor," Tristan said, moving over to his porthole. "Yes, it was. We're moving."

Casey put her face up to her porthole again and watched the line of trees in the distance. She could see the island grow smaller and smaller. "Tristan, we're going the wrong way!" she said. "We're moving away from Libertalia! Where are they taking us?"

Tristan let his breath out. "Out to sea," he said. "The captain must have made his decision."

≈

They sailed away from land for about half an hour before they finally heard someone coming down the dark passageway. Casey was a nervous wreck the entire time, wondering what the captain had decided to do, how she could escape, how she would get back to the door, and how she would recover her things. Tristan repeatedly tried to reassure her by telling her that he would figure something out, but she didn't see how. They were locked up and trapped on a ship miles and miles from land. There was absolutely no place to go.

The same men who had brought them down into their cells emerged from the darkness. Their grimaces were wide, curling up the corners of their mouths and baring their black teeth. Their eyes gleamed with anticipation; they already knew what was about to happen. Casey could see it in their faces. They were excited for her misfortune and were looking forward to witnessing it. Captain Scabbard was apparently right. These pirates didn't care a bit that she was a young girl.

"Let's go, girly," said Peg Leg Pete, unlocking the cell doors. "Your time has come. And you, lad, you get to watch."

His wooden stump clunked along the floor as they led Casey and Tristan back up on deck. All the pirates gathered again, and Captain Scabbard waited in front of them. Casey scanned the water for Greybeard's ship, but it was nowhere in sight. That was probably a good sign. At least they weren't going to turn her over to him. However, there wasn't even a trace of a smile on Captain Scabbard's face when the pair was put in front of him. He was dead serious.

"I think we're far enough out to sea now for what I aim to do," he said. "Aye, and ye know I hate to do it too with ye being a little lass and all, but it has to be done, ye see. I can't have ye going round bewitching my men. Ye already got to Tristan here, but he's a youngin too, and his mum'll straighten him out. And he be lucky that I'm fond of his mum, or he'd be going with ye."

"I'm not a witch, sir," pleaded Casey. "I swear to you. I'm not."

"I can't trust ye, lass. The decision has been made."

"What do you mean to do with me?" asked Casey.

"Well, I decided to be easy on ye and not keelhaul ye or run ye through with a sword," he said kindly, as if he were doing her a favor. "Yer just gonna walk the plank. Maybe ye'll survive, and maybe ye won't. Maybe there're sharks down there, and maybe there ain't. I'm giving ye a fightin' chance. What happens after ye walk the plank, I don't care to know."

"Some chance," mumbled Casey.

With a nod from Captain Scabbard, Cutthroat Bill seized Casey's arm and pulled her forward, leading her to the wooden plank that stretched out over the side of the ship. She looked back at Tristan with wide, pleading eyes. Red Eye and Coldblood were holding his arms. He returned her gaze and silently mouthed the words, "Don't worry." Casey looked ahead of her again as they approached the plank and thought, *Ha! Don't worry, he says. That's a good one. What's he gonna do now? I'm a goner for sure.* She began to think that all of his reassurances meant nothing. He had just said them to make her feel better.

She stopped at the step leading up to the plank and looked at Cutthroat Bill. His smile made all the scars on his face twist into a gnarled lump. He was definitely taking pleasure in this. He drew a long sword from his side and put the tip against Casey's back. She felt the sharp point prick her skin along her spine.

"Walk, girly, or I'll run ye through meself," he said.

Casey stepped up onto the plank and walked out to the edge. It was a bit of a fall down to the water, but that was nothing. She had jumped from the cliffs in the jungle last summer and loved it after she had gotten over her fear. What she was afraid of now was sharks or drowning. She could swim quite well, but for how long? There was no land in sight. And it wouldn't matter anyway if a shark did come along. She felt the warm breeze against her face and looked down into the water. It was still crystal clear, and there were no signs of any sharks in the immediate area. She turned her head back to take one last look at Tristan.

"He can't help ye now," said Cutthroat Bill. "Don't make me come out there, girly. Now, get to jumping."

Casey turned back to the water and stepped off the edge of the plank. She hit the water in a matter of seconds and plunged down several feet below the surface. It was warm and quiet, and she lingered there for a moment before starting to kick and paddle her way back up.

When she broke the surface, she wiped the water from her face and looked back up at the ship as she treaded water. The whole motley gang of pirates was staring over the railing at her, with the exception of Captain Scabbard. They were laughing with their rotten mouths wide open and waving their hands.

"Good-bye, girly! Hope ye don't get eaten up! Hope ye can swim for a long, long time!"

Tristan was there as well, but he wasn't laughing. He was mouthing something to her again, but she couldn't make out what it was. The ship's main deck was too high above her. A minute or so later, the pirates dispersed. When the ship began to move away, only Tristan remained, clutching the railing and watching her grow smaller as they sailed away.

Left alone in the middle of the ocean, Casey turned in a circle, searching the horizon in each direction for any sign of land. No luck. All she could see was blue water and blue sky. Even if she were to attempt to swim to land, she wouldn't know which direction to go. She was disoriented from being locked up in the cell and wasn't sure if the ship was headed back to Libertalia or further out to sea. She could hear the pirates' shouts and laughter echoing across the water for a little while, but as the ship became a small dot in the distance, it died away and left her with only the sound of the wind above her and the waves lapping around her. It was strange not to hear any birds or insects or small animals scuttling in the bushes. It was a feeling of complete isolation, complete helplessness.

The sun beat down on her face as she switched between treading water and floating on her back. She felt like she must have been at it for more than a half hour and was beginning to grow tired. Luckily, she still hadn't seen any signs of sharks, but she wasn't sure how long she could keep it up. Even the periods of floating took a little effort, and her arms and legs were growing weary. She wondered what would happen if she drowned. She didn't have much faith in the "you can't die because you're not a character in the book" theory right about then, and she didn't want to find out. If it were true, she imagined herself drowning and then waking up just as tired as she was before and then drowning over and over again. That was too terrible to even consider. And what would happen if she didn't get out by midnight? That was starting to look inevitable. Her watch was not waterproof, and it had stopped working when she plunged into the water. It had stopped at quarter to eleven, which still gave her some time, being that time was different there. It allowed her to spend an entire day or more inside a book while only a few hours passed in the real world, but she'd need to find a way back soon. This was the worst situation she had ever gotten herself into. And she was all alone.

As terrible thoughts continued to rush through her head, her body became weaker by the minute. Only pure determination to free Uncle Walt and get back to her family kept her going. She refused to give up hope yet, but she knew her strength was waning. She kept watch on the horizon in each direction, looking for something—anything—that could help her. A passing ship or even a floating piece of wood would come in handy, but luck didn't seem to be on her side at the moment.

Her arms and legs burned with exhaustion, and she had to rest. She switched to the floating position and closed her eyes. She took deep, slow breaths and thought, *That's it. I'm done for. I can't go on any longer. I'm just going to let myself sink down into the silence. I'm sorry, Uncle Walt. I'm sorry, Mom and Dad and Ryan and even Samantha. I'm sorry.*

But then something reached her ears. The sound was very faint, and she wasn't sure if she'd even heard it at all. Maybe the sun and the exhaustion were making her delirious, playing tricks with her senses. She strained her ears, listening hard. There it was again, and it was a bit louder this time. Casey popped back upright, turning in circles to find where the sound was coming from.

"Caaaseeey!"

She heard it distinctly that time and turned toward it. A small black dot hovered in the distance, and she began to swim, ignoring the deep burn in her limbs. It was Tristan. It had to be Tristan. A swell of hope surged through her, and she pushed herself harder, laughing and yelling at the same time. "Tristan! Over here! I'm over here! Tristan!"

Tears of joy and relief streamed down her face as the figure grew closer, and she realized that it really was him. He had come back for her.

He was rowing a small boat, but it wasn't the one they had taken earlier that day. He pulled up alongside of her and grabbed her arms, dragging her into the boat. Casey laid flat on the bottom, unable to move, laughing and crying at the same time.

"Oh my God, Tristan. I thought I was done for. Thank you, thank you, thank you for coming back. How did you get away?"

"I told you not to worry," he said with a smile. "They didn't lock me up again. As soon as they went below deck for grub, I took your bag, slipped past the lookout, and dropped this boat into the water. All the ships have one to get to shore when there's no docks."

Casey suddenly had the energy to sit up. "My bag? You got my bag too?" It was on the floor of the boat next to Tristan's leg. She sprang up and hugged him, rocking the boat and almost tipping it over. "You really are the best! Thank you so much!"

"Okay, okay," Tristan said, trying to steady the boat. "Calm down, or we'll both end up shark bait."

"Sorry, just got a little excited," Casey said, taking a seat opposite Tristan. "I hate to do this to you because I'm sure you're tired, but my time is running a little short. I've got to get home."

"You didn't think we were gonna stay here all day, did you?" Tristan said. "I'll get you home. My arms have plenty of strength left in them."

Tristan took off toward Libertalia, rowing hard. Every so often, when his arms got tired, Casey relieved him and rowed for a bit. After about forty-five minutes, they could see the island in the distance, but they caught sight of something else too. The last thing they wanted to see. Greybeard's ship was floating offshore.

"Maybe he won't see us," Casey said hopefully.

"Maybe," Tristan said, but there wasn't an ounce of hope in his voice. He changed directions and started pulling even harder on the oars. "I won't be able to bring you back to Libertalia. I'm gonna have to drop you off on the other side of the island."

"Are you sure there's even anyone on the ship?" Casey asked. "Maybe everyone's on shore, and we can just go into the woods outside of town, like this morning."

Before Tristan could answer, they heard a distant *boom* and a whistling sound, like wind rushing through a narrow canyon. A few seconds later, a large black cannonball hit the water about ten feet from their boat, sending up a spray that soaked them both.

Casey screamed and shouted, "Row faster, Tristan! It's moving! Greybeard's ship is moving this way! Drop me off anywhere. I don't care!"

"Don't worry," Tristan said. "I'll get you to the island. Just pray that one of those cannonballs doesn't get us first."

Casey had decided to go back through the door to real world since it was starting to get close to midnight instead of investigating the hidden door as she had planned. But now, there was no way she would get back to the regular door in time if Tristan was going to drop her off on the other side of the island. She pulled the chart out of her backpack as cannonballs continued to drop into the water around them. She covered it with her body as best she could to keep it dry. It would do her no good if it was unreadable. Water showered down on her back as she hunched over the chart. She checked the map for the red dot. Yes, she would be close to it. It looked like it wasn't far off the beach—just a short walk or run into the woods. But what would she do if she ended up someplace she didn't know and still couldn't get to the regular door in time? Could she even find it at all? She'd still be in just as bad a position as she was now.

She put the chart away and looked back. Greybeard's ship was gaining on them, and she could see the dark pirate at the helm, perfectly still and watching them with a deadly look. Maybe she wouldn't be in quite as bad a position after all if she went through the hidden door. At least she wouldn't have a dreaded pirate pursuing her anymore, but it really didn't matter because she had no choice. The hidden door was her only chance.

Tristan's face was flushed, and sweat streamed off his forehead as he ran the boat ashore. He hopped out, dragged it up on the sand, and plopped down, breathing hard.

Casey knelt beside him and hugged him. "I'm so sorry for getting you into this mess," she said. "Will you be okay? What will they do to you?"

Tristan brushed the sweat-soaked hair out of his eyes, revealing the turquoise blue of the sea. "I'll be fine. They won't do anything to me. I'll hide out in the woods tonight and make my way home tomorrow. They won't touch me once I'm with my mum."

Casey stood up and put her backpack on her shoulders. Greybeard's ship was only a hundred yards offshore, and she could hear the pirates yelling from the railing. They were beginning to drop the side boat so they could row to shore. Then, a shot rang out through the air and they heard a *thump* in a nearby tree.

"Time to go!" said Tristan, getting to his feet.

They ran for the woods, and when they were safely beneath the canopy of trees, Casey grabbed Tristan's hand and stopped him. "Thank you so much, Tristan. Thank you for everything. And promise me you'll get away from this place someday and become something great."

"I promise," he said. "Don't forget that I'm the smartest one here. You don't have to worry about me." He released his hand from hers and started to back away. "Now, you better get going. Hurry!"

Tristan turned and sprinted off into the deep woods.

Casey turned to her left and jogged for a few minutes through the trees. She could still hear the pirates' voices. They must have been on the beach or maybe even in the woods already. She picked up her pace and adjusted her direction a little more inland. In another minute, she reached a small clearing. What she found there wasn't just a door. There were two doors, side by side, suspended with nothing around them.

Casey stood in front of them, contemplating. "Two doors? How do you like that? Which one do I choose? Does it matter? Do they take me to different places?"

She decided to use the eeny-meeny-miney-moe technique, and it landed on the door to the right. She took the key out of its box, assuming that was what it was for, but when she put it in the lock, it didn't work. She tried the other door. Same thing.

That's weird. If it's not for the hidden doors, then what is it for?

Some rustling in the trees behind her reminded her that she *was* in a bit of a hurry. Twigs were breaking, and angry, out-of-breath pirate voices were coming closer. Casey put the key back and took out her regular bookshop key, praying that it would work. She held her breath as she slipped it into the lock of the door on the right. To her great relief, it turned. She hurried through and shut the door, leaving the deep green forest of Madagascar behind her. She had learned over time that the characters in the books didn't seem to care about the doors. They just kind of accepted them being there and never tried to go through them. She thought that maybe part of the magic was to keep everyone where they were supposed to be—and that was a very good thing. If that weren't the case, Casey was certain that these pirates would've chopped their way through it to get to her.

She turned around to see where she was and almost stumbled as she found herself in deep, soft, hot desert sand. She immediately recognized the tall, pointed structures in the distance and realized she'd been there before.

Chapter 7
AMUN AND THE AMULET

Casey was standing in the deep orange sands of ancient Egypt. The title of the book was *Under the Eye of Ra,* and she had been there the previous summer. She had become friends with Amun, the son of the Pharaoh, but she had no time for reunions now. She knew where the door to the real world was, and it was about half a mile away.

Her watch was still broken and useless, but she was sure it must be close to midnight. At least, she hoped it was close to midnight and not past it yet. She wasted no time and broke into a run as best she could through the deep, soft sand. It made her body feel slow and heavy as her feet struggled for traction and kicked up clouds of sand behind her. Already tired from treading water in the ocean and running from pirates, she reached the door and collapsed on her knees in pure exhaustion, breathing so hard that she felt like she would never catch her breath again. Before she could go through the door, however, she had to do something with the box she had dug up in Madagascar.

First, she checked her backpack to make sure it was still there. It was. So, that was good news. It meant that she could take things that she found in the books with her through the hidden doors, from book to book, but she still wouldn't be able to take anything out to the real world. She had to leave the box and its precious contents there.

She took out her shovel and started digging furiously in the sand next to the door. She only went down about a foot and then placed the box with the Moonstone and the key into the hole. She packed the sand back on top of it and prayed that no one would find it until she came back. Then, she took out her bookshop key and opened the door. She stuck her arm through first to make sure it didn't disappear. That would tell her if it was past midnight or not. She would have laughed with joy if she had any breath left in her as she saw her flesh gleaming with sweat on the other side of the threshold. She stepped the rest of the way through and stood in the darkness of the bookshop.

Her legs felt rubbery and wobbly. A ten-minute walk home seemed almost impossible at the moment, so she turned on a lamp and sat in one of the big, comfy chairs. The clock on the wall read five minutes to midnight. She put her head back against the soft material, but she dared not close her eyes. She knew she would be asleep in a matter of seconds, and she had to be back in her own bed before morning. It felt like a month had gone by since she left for Oktoberfest only a few hours earlier. Her body felt like it had been hit by a truck. She honestly didn't think she had ever been that tired in her life. She sat there for a few minutes, letting her legs recover and trying to clear her mind. She'd have all day tomorrow to ponder everything; right now, she just wanted peace and sleep.

When she thought she could manage to walk, she left the shop in an almost half-conscious state and dragged herself home. She threw her shovel on the ground around the side of the house and practically crawled up the stairs to her room. She lost consciousness the moment her head hit the pillow, and she slept like the dead—fully clothed and completely immobile—until the light of day.

≈

When Casey awoke late Sunday morning, her arms and legs still ached. She snuggled down under her covers and let the events of the night before fill her mind. She now had a whole new set of questions and mysteries to solve, on top of the other ones she hadn't even figured out yet. What was this new key for if it wasn't for the hidden doors? Were there two doors at each location of the red dots? And if so, did they lead to different places? She tried to remember if there were two doors on the other side where she had come through into ancient Egypt. She thought she remembered seeing one there, just as there had been in the *Libertalia* book, but she was so frantic to get back to the real world that she hadn't paid attention.

And then there was the Moonstone. Now that she knew that it really did exist, she would have to figure out Miz Luna's message. Where was its proper place, and how would she find it? She had also said something about finding protection in ancient sands and finding her might in a dark cave. It clicked as soon as the words entered her mind. Ancient sands. She was standing in ancient sands last night. That had to be what she was talking about. But what kind of protection and where? Ancient Egypt was a big place. She was rapidly coming up with way more questions than she had answers, and she was beginning to get frustrated.

One step at a time, Casey thought. For starters, she would go back into the Egypt book and find Amun. Maybe he could help. She also had to retrieve the box and figure out what to do with it. Not being able to bring things out to the real world was quite inconvenient.

In the midst of her pondering, Casey heard something at her window that made her throw her covers off and sit straight up. Rain. Fat droplets of water were softly tapping on the glass, and the sky was a misty gray. She stared at it in disbelief. Could things possibly get any worse? The magic doesn't work in the rain. No moonlight. If it didn't stop by nighttime, she wouldn't be going anywhere. She had planned on breaking her own rule of not going on school nights. This was an emergency that couldn't wait for the weekends, but as it looked outside now, it seemed she would be well rested for school on Monday morning.

Casey headed downstairs for something to eat and found everyone at home, just finishing up a Sunday pancake breakfast. Her mother was at the table, doing a crossword puzzle and picking at a pancake on the plate next to her. Her father was also at the table, reading the paper with one foot propped up on the opposite knee. He was obviously in relax mode. Ryan and Samantha were on the couch, arguing over what to watch.

"Good morning, sleepyhead," her mother said. "I guess someone had a good time at Oktoberfest last night."

Casey rubbed her eyes and tried to put on her best "nothing is wrong" voice. "Yeah, it was really fun. We ate so much that it was ridiculous. And Nick actually ate deep-fried frog's legs. It was gross."

"Who puked?" asked Ryan, turning his head around to look at her.

"No one," Casey answered. "Can you believe that? And we went on all the rides too."

"Impressive," said Ryan. "My buddy, Danny, bragged about his iron stomach and then went on the swings and puked all over the place. It was hilarious. You shoulda seen his face."

"Well, now that my appetite is ruined, I think I'll skip the pancakes," Casey said. "Thanks a lot, Ry."

"Really, Ryan?" Samantha said. "Do you have to talk about puking at breakfast? Danny is an idiot anyway. He'll do anything for attention."

"Sorry, squirt," Ryan said to Casey. "Didn't mean to kill your appetite, but it was funny!"

"I'm sure it was," said Casey. "And I'm just kidding. You know I'm always ready to eat. Mom, any pancakes left?"

With a full belly and the rain still coming down outside, Casey thought it would be a good day to do some research. She hopped on the family computer and started pulling up any information she could find on ancient Egypt. Miz Luna had said she would find protection in ancient sands, so what did the ancient Egyptians use for protection? Every site she went to said the same thing: amulets or talismans. And there were a lot of them. They seemed to have an amulet for everything, a different one to protect each part of the body, even their throats! Some of them were formed in the shape of body parts, and some were in the shapes of gods, but most of them were in the shapes of animals. They were made as rings, bracelets, necklaces, or figurines to carry. One in particular stood out from the rest and kept popping up everywhere she looked. They revered the scarab more than any other and used it for special purposes, including being buried with the pharaohs.

In essence, it was a beetle that they held sacred. When it was depicted in an amulet, it was supposed to protect the heart, and in a more general sense, would ward off evil. Sometimes it was shown as just the beetle itself, but other times, it was a winged beetle holding a round disc between its two front legs. The wings were painted blue to represent the Nile river, and flecks of yellow represented the desert sand. The disc was orange to represent the sun god, Ra. It was a stunning piece of jewelry. Casey hoped that was what she was looking for. She wouldn't mind having that strung around her neck.

She hoped Amun would have one—or know where to get one. He *was* the son of the Pharaoh after all, and he should be able to get whatever he wanted. He had proved it when he used his clout to get them past the guard into the pyramid of King Khufu, which was forbidden to anyone but the pharaoh.

As for the other parts of Miz Luna's message, those mysteries would have to wait for another day. After taking a break to watch some TV, it was nearing nine o'clock. The rain was still coming down outside. As much as Casey was anxious about getting on with things, she was still achy and tired from the night before. It was probably better that the rain was keeping her home. She would be ready to go at it again Monday night, assuming that the rain was going to stop by then. After that, it was probably going to get tough adventuring by night and getting up for school the next day. Not to mention staying awake in class all day. But, she had to do it. She had to get Uncle Walt out of there.

≈

All throughout school the next day, in every class and at lunch, kids were talking about Oktoberfest—who ate what and who went on what rides and who puked or didn't puke and did you see those silly polka dancers? Casey interjected here and there, but she kept her eye on the clock, which moved ever so slowly. *Doesn't it always when you're in school?*

She was distracted all day long by worries about her box being discovered. She tried to tell herself not to worry. No one would find it. The characters never messed with the doors, and it was buried right next to one. It would be fine. As hard as she tried, the thought kept creeping back in. She had a feeling that if she lost the Moonstone and the key, all would be lost. They must have been buried for a reason, and they must be crucial elements for something.

She couldn't wait for the school day to end and for night to come so she could get to Egypt to get that box back in her possession. As she stared out the window of her fifth period science class, at least one worry was lifted from her mind. It had stopped raining and the sky was clearing.

Casey was looking forward to seeing Amun again too. The prince was fun and adventurous and ready to take on anything. He wasn't afraid of trouble and was a little mischievous as well. Thinking of him made her think of another friend she hadn't seen in a long time. Kamari was much like Amun, except for the mischievous part, and was wise beyond his years. He lived in the jungles of Africa in the first book she had ever gone into.

Kamari was by far her favorite character. She had befriended him immediately and shared a bond with him that was only rivaled in the real world by her brother. She could tell Kamari anything, and he would listen intently to everything she had to say. She had told him all about her bully situation last summer, and he always encouraged her and gave her good advice. He generally just made her feel better. She couldn't help but feel better when she was around him. He wasn't afraid of anything. He had protected her from a giant snake and a ferocious lion. And he had taught her how to conquer her fear. She truly missed him. As soon as this whole thing was over, the first thing she was going to do was pay a visit to Kamari.

≈

The moonlight shined overhead as Casey walked to Moonglow's. Having finished her homework quickly and gotten in a nap after school, she was ready to go do some digging and find some ancient amulets. She had retrieved her shovel from the side of the house and zipped it into her backpack, which was already beginning to wear. Some of the edges were frayed. She thought of how much it had been through and how far she still had to go. It had survived the destruction of a city and being hijacked by pirates. Maybe it was her lucky backpack. She didn't care how worn it was; she was sticking with it till the end.

As soon as she felt the soft Egyptian sand under her feet and the scorching hot sun begin to blaze overhead, Casey went to work. She found the spot near the door and dug it up with her trusty shovel. That was something else that was turning out to be quite useful. She just might have to keep it with her all the time. *You never know when you're going to need a shovel.*

As she had hoped, the box was still there. She peeked inside to make sure everything was there and sighed with relief as she placed it in her backpack. She felt much better having it in her possession. It renewed her hope that things were progressing and that she was on the right track. She would have to figure out something else to do with it each night when she exited the books. She couldn't keep burying it in different places. That felt way too risky; even if she buried it near a door every night, it would drive her crazy all day at home, wondering if it was okay. No, it was too important. She would have to figure out something else.

Casey headed to the city. It was just as magnificent as she remembered. Low stone buildings, the color of sand, sprawled out from the three great pyramids, and the Sphinx loomed overhead.

She would find Amun in the great temple with the tall obelisk in the middle of the city—unless he was fishing in the Nile. She had met him the first time on his way home from the river.

She gazed at the vividly painted scenes and hieroglyphics covering every wall as she made her way to the temple. They still amazed her as much as they had before. If only everyone could see them that way, in their original state, rather than faded bits and pieces here and there. She passed the obelisk and walked through the massive stone pillars of the entryway to the temple. It was completely quiet, and there was no one in sight. She walked farther back and called Amun's name as loud as she dared. Her voice echoed through the halls as she passed through the vast rooms. "Amun! Where are you? Amun! Are you here?"

Corridors broke off on both sides after every other room. If she didn't stay straight, she'd be lost in no time. She heard footsteps running toward her from the right. Casey quickly ducked behind a chair, just in case it was someone she didn't know. She had met Amun's mother, the queen, but she hadn't met his father, the pharaoh. She assumed that there were guards around too. In jeans and a t-shirt, she didn't want to run into anyone she didn't know. They would most assuredly think her a spy or an evil being of some sort—and who knew what they would do. She had already experienced what pirates did with strangers, and that was enough. She had no desire to find out what ancient Egyptians would do.

The footsteps reached the end of the corridor, and then they stopped. A few tense, silent seconds went by before a voice broke the silence. "Casey?"

Casey recognized the young boy's voice immediately. She popped up from behind the chair. "Amun!" she said with a big smile.

He smiled back and ran over to her. "I thought I heard your voice. I'm so glad you're here!"

His smile was as bright as the sun. His hair was jet black, his skin was bronze, and he was dressed in a white belted tunic with golden sandals that wound all the way up to his knees, his usual garb. It was strange to imagine wearing the same thing day after day. He didn't seem to mind though.

"Remember when I was here last time?" said Casey. "We talked about using your influence as the future king to have some adventures?"

"Yes," he said with a grin. "What do you have in mind?"

"Well, I need something. I need protection, and it's gotta be the most powerful protection there is. I've heard about these amulets you guys have here, and the one that looks like a beetle seems pretty good."

Amun thought for a moment. "This *will* be an adventure. That is certain. Amulets you can find anywhere—from any marketplace vendor, any size, any type you want—but they are meaningless. People believe in them because they want to. If you want a true amulet, you have to get one that has had a certain ritual performed on it by a priest. A true priest who was ordained by my father. As you know, the pharaoh is the living embodiment of Ra, and only he can ordain a priest."

He hesitated and then moved them further into the room. He began to whisper. "Now, if you want the most powerful amulet of all, yes, it is the winged scarab. And you must get one that has been buried with a pharaoh and placed there by the pharaoh's high priest."

"And I'm guessing this is a big no-no," Casey said. "Messing with the mummy of a dead king."

"Yes," said Amun. "It is absolutely forbidden, and it is the worst crime you can commit. It is disrespectful to the dead king, and I do not know what will happen. And, besides that, if we get caught—"

"So, the answer is no? I don't blame you for being afraid, and I definitely don't want to get you in trouble. I'll do it by myself ... if you could just tell me where to go."

"Oh, I didn't say I wasn't going to do it," Amun said, his grin widening. "You know I'm not afraid of trouble, but we must be very careful."

"Thank you, Amun!" Casey said, hugging him.

"Do not thank me yet," he said with a concerned look. "You can thank me if we survive. Let's go before my mother finds me."

Casey wasn't too worried. She knew all the mummy and afterlife stuff was part of their culture, their belief that the life of the pharaohs continued after death when they went to join the gods. She wasn't superstitious that way. It was just a mummy. What could possibly happen? Then again, it was fiction. Anything could happen.

Amun led Casey toward the three great pyramids. Everyone they passed was busy with their day-to-day lives. The men were painting and carving scenes into the stone walls and monuments, or they were selling wares in the busy marketplace. The women were buying those wares or coming back from the Nile with baskets of laundry and jugs of water. It was a busy city, and Amun and Casey floated through unnoticed.

"Are we going into one of the pyramids again?" Casey asked.

"Not this time," Amun said. "We're going someplace older—into the tomb of an ancient king. The amulet there will be much more powerful because the magic in it is so old. His name was King Nekhebu, and from what I know of him, you do not want to be his enemy. He was a brutal warrior who slashed down his foes without mercy."

Casey began to feel a little uneasy. She remembered when she had seen the sarcophagus of King Khufu inside the pyramid. The face painted on the lid seemed to bore into her soul so that she was afraid to even touch it, and now she had to retrieve something that was buried with a long-dead, fiercely brutal king. Maybe this wasn't such a good idea after all, but there was no turning back now. She needed that protection. Miz Luna had said so, and she aimed to get it.

When they reached the edge of the city, the three great pyramids and the sphinx were directly in front of them, but they went right and headed for a couple of large statues Casey could see rising out of the sand in the distance. As they drew near, the statues became more than large. They were enormous. Everything in ancient Egypt was larger than life. They didn't do anything on a small scale. Their motto seemed to be "go big or go home," and it was one of the things Casey loved about it.

Two massive seated stone pharaohs guarded the entrance to the tomb. They wore the headdress and fake beard that every pharaoh wore, and they sat silently with their hands on their knees, watching for any intruders who might enter the tomb. Between them was a door; on either side, hieroglyphics had been etched into the stone and outlined with a square.

"What does this say?" Casey asked.

"It's a warning," Amun replied, his face turning deadly serious. "It says, 'Beware the wrath of King Nekhebu, any who dare enter here.' Many of the kings, especially the ancient ones, put curses on their tombs to keep anyone from disturbing them or trying to rob them. And this king, being so old and fierce, I'm sure cast the most powerful curses there are. That's why I said *if* we survive. No one dares to even come near this tomb. Are you sure you still want to do this?"

"No," Casey croaked. The word caught in her throat, but she cleared it and forced the words out solidly. "But I have no choice. I'm not turning back. And I still understand if you don't want to come with me."

"I'm here until the bitter end," Amun said. "Come on. Let's see what this king's got."

They pushed open the door and entered a wide room lit by torches. It was completely bare, except for one statue in the center, reaching from floor to ceiling. It was a seated pharaoh, just like the ones outside, but the face was different, and it was brightly painted, making it seem lifelike. The pharaoh's face was deeply lined, with thin hard lips and furrowed brows, giving him an expression of anger. His deep-set green eyes were outlined in heavy black, exaggerating the ferocity even more.

"Is that King Nekhebu?" Casey asked.

"Yes."

"Oh boy. I think we are in trouble," Casey said, staring at the statue. She glanced around the rest of the room. "What do we do now? And how are these torches burning if no one ever comes in here?"

"I don't know," said Amun. "Let's check the other side."

As soon as they walked around the statue, they saw a door on the far wall. Behind it, a dark passageway sloped down for several hundred feet.

Amun grabbed a torch off the wall and insisted on going first. That was perfectly fine with Casey. The passageway was just wide enough that if Casey stretched her arms out, she could almost touch the walls with her fingertips. She kept her hands to herself and tried to step as lightly as she could for fear of setting something off. She didn't want to disturb even the smallest pebble.

As they neared the end of the passageway, a bright light in the room ahead was shifting and flickering. It was as if something was on fire, but there was no smell of smoke. They came to a halt before they reached the edge of the light.

"I don't like this, Amun," whispered Casey. "I don't like this one bit."

"Neither do I. Wait here. I'm going to peek around the corner."

Casey held her breath as she watched Amun creep up to the edge of the passageway. He quickly popped his head around the corner and then walked back to her with a puzzled look.

"What did you see?" asked Casey anxiously.

"Fire," said Amun. "A wall of fire."

"What?"

The chamber they entered was as large and wide as the one above, but this one had a wall of flames running through its center. It reached from floor to ceiling and from wall to wall, dividing the room in half and keeping them from reaching the other side. Through the shimmering, shifting wall of red and orange, they could see the hazy outline of another door on the far wall of the chamber. The fire looked impenetrable, and there was no way around it. The flames sizzled and popped, but oddly there was no smell, and no black or white puffs of smoke either. Heat emanated from it, but it didn't seem as ragingly hot as a wall of fire should be. The walls of the chamber were covered with pictures of people, in the classic angular style, being burned by fire, engulfed in flames, and writhing on the ground in agony or running away with their bodies ablaze.

"What do you make of this?" Casey asked.

"I'm not sure," said Amun. "There is a door on the other side, so there must be a way to get there. The trick is to figure out how. Let's look along the walls and floor to see if we can find anything."

They searched every inch of wall and floor they could reach, but they found nothing. They came back together in the center of the room and stood before the fire.

"I'm beginning to think this isn't real fire," Amun said. "It's a trick to keep people out."

"I don't know," said Casey. "Those pictures on the wall are enough to scare me away. And the fire looks real enough. It's hot when you get close to it, but it *is* weird that there's no smoke."

"Yes. No smoke and no way around it."

"So, what are you saying?"

"I'm saying we go through it."

"Ha. Yeah, right. You must be crazy."

"No, I'm serious, Casey. I've learned enough about our past kings that I can guess how they would've thought. And I bet this one is saving the real challenges for later. This is the easy one … to eliminate the cowards."

"This is the easy one? Isn't there another amulet we can get somewhere else that isn't booby-trapped all the way there?"

"You said you wanted the best, and this one will be the best. Do you want it or not?"

"I do," Casey said heavily.

"Well then, I'll go first."

Casey didn't argue. She bit her lip and twisted her fingers together as Amun stepped back a few paces. Visions of him being burned to a crisp flashed before her eyes. She tried not to look at the pictures on the wall.

Amun took a deep breath and pushed off at full speed. He ran straight at the wall of fire, without hesitation and without looking back.

Just before he made contact, Casey had to fight the urge to scream out his name and tell him to stop. She somehow managed to hold it inside as Amun made contact with the flames. For a brief second, he lit up like the night sky on the Fourth of July, and then he was through. He came to a stop on the other side of the flames and turned around to face Casey.

"See? I told you!" he shouted. "I'm fine! I didn't feel a thing! Come on!"

Casey nodded and smiled weakly. She started walking backward slowly. She wanted as much of a running start as she could get. "You can do this," she told herself quietly. "There's nothing to it. Look at Amun over there. He's fine. You'll be fine." She breathed deeply several times and then pushed off. She brought herself up to full speed and almost stopped herself right before she hit the wall, but she forced her legs to keep going. She could feel the heat from the flames a half a second before she hit them and thought she would be incinerated for sure. She closed her eyes tight and blasted through the fire. The next thing she knew, she was tumbling to the ground on top of Amun.

"You made it!" Amun said. "You can open your eyes. You're okay."

Casey opened her eyes and looked down. Everything looked completely normal. No burn marks or singed clothing, and she hadn't felt a thing—just as Amun had said.

"Whoa. That was weird," she said, picking herself up off the ground. "Sorry. I guess I ran right into you."

"Don't worry about it," said Amun, smoothing out his tunic. "You were as bright as Ra when you came through the flames. It was quite a sight."

"I know. I saw you light up too. And I guess we'll get to see it again on the way out. Wonderful."

Amun laughed. "It wasn't really that bad. Come on. Let's see what's next."

≈

They opened the door on the other side of the chamber and found another dark passageway that led down to another level.

Amun had tossed the torch aside on the other side of the fire, and they decided to go on without it since neither of them wanted to have to run through the flames any more than they absolutely had to. They dragged one hand along the smooth rock wall as the passageway gently sloped down. It zigzagged a few times and seemed to be longer than the first one. When they finally reached the end, they paused so Amun could take a peek inside the next room.

He looked back at Casey and waved her on. "It's a map room. Stay close behind me. I don't know what tricks Nekhebu has up his sleeve for this one."

Casey turned the corner and found a long, narrow chamber lined with torches that widened at the opposite end, like a giant capital T. A walkway pieced together with large slabs of stone ran up the center and was surrounded by water on either side. At the other end, there was an unfinished model of a city. Little stone buildings and monuments were scattered on the floor next to it. There was another door on the far wall.

They walked slowly and carefully down the walkway, pausing every few steps, waiting for something to happen. Casey looked down into the water. It was shallow and clear and threw shimmery reflections upon the walls that, mixed with the flickering torch light, made the room seem to almost move.

"This place is making me paranoid," Casey said. "I hate not knowing what's going to happen."

"Yes. It does make a person uneasy," said Amun, stepping lightly from stone to stone.

When they reached the other side, Casey walked around the miniature city to try the door. She pushed as hard as she could, digging her feet into the floor, but they only slipped out from underneath her, causing her to land on her knees.

"No good," she said, hopping up on her feet and rubbing her knees.

Amun chuckled.

"What?" asked Casey. "That's really hard stone."

"I didn't think it would open," said Amun. "He would never make it that easy."

Casey came back and stood with Amun in front of the little city. It covered an area as big and wide as her driveway back home. If she tiptoed through it, she could pretend she was walking up and down the stone streets, but something was missing.

"Where are the three pyramids?" asked Casey.

"They weren't built yet," said Amun. "This is a map of the city in King Nekhebu's time. The city was different then, and some of these things don't exist anymore." He paused for a moment. "I'm guessing he wants us to finish it since there are a pile of buildings over there and empty spaces all throughout the map."

"And you're thinking that this isn't just a fun jigsaw puzzle, right?" Casey asked nervously.

"Exactly."

"But you do know where everything goes, right?"

"Not exactly."

They both stood in silence for a few minutes, wondering what the consequences might be for making a mistake. Casey was picturing venomous snakes crawling out of the water—or the king himself materializing out of thin air to strike them down. She shivered at the thought.

Finally, Amun said, "But I have seen paintings of the old city before. I will do my best."

"And we will hope for the best," Casey said. "I'll help you. Tell me what goes where."

Amun grabbed an obelisk and a statue of Ra. He handed the obelisk to Casey. "I remember where these go," he said. "Put that one in the empty spot over there by that temple."

There was a little square outline that fit the base of the obelisk perfectly. Casey gently clicked it into place as Amun did the same with his mini falcon-headed god of the sun. Then they waited a few seconds. Nothing. Still quiet. With a brief sigh of relief, they moved on to the next two. Amun chose the pieces he was sure of first. The monuments and various statues of gods and pharaohs were easier to remember and place. When he was finished with those, there were ten pieces left. He picked up a small rectangular building and stood in front of the map, carefully considering. "The ones that are left are just random insignificant buildings," he said. "I have no idea where they go."

Casey stood next to him. "Well, you can kind of tell the shape of things by the spaces that are left. I see three possible spots that would fit that type of building."

"I see them too, but which one?"

"I guess it's time to find out the consequences," Casey said, glancing warily at Amun. "Unless we happen to get lucky. I don't think we'll get lucky ten times in a row, do you?"

Amun shook his head. "No, I don't."

He stepped over a few houses to one of the empty spaces. He looked up at Casey and gently placed the building into the rectangular outline. A sudden rumble under their feet made the whole room tremble.

Casey instantly thought of Atlantis. "Oh no. Not again!" She started backing away from the map. A shattering, crumbling sound came from behind her.

"Casey! Stop!" yelled Amun.

She turned around to see one of the stone slabs in the walkway falling to pieces into a dark abyss below. She tried to reverse direction so fast that she slipped and fell on her butt. She scrambled to her feet and hurried back to the edge of the map.

"That's definitely not the right place, Amun!" she said frantically, but he already had the building in another spot and was going for the third. When he placed it in the last possible space, everything went still and quiet.

"Luck is not on our side," said Amun, looking a bit more worried.

"I don't like these consequences," said Casey. "There's a deep black nothingness under here. And who knows what's in there or if it even has a bottom!"

"Maybe it's an entrance to the Duat. And if so, we certainly don't want to fall into it."

"What's the Duat?"

"It's the underworld. The god Anubis lives down there, as well as some others, but it's not the gods you have to worry about. There are also evil beings. Monstrous spirits that you really don't want to meet."

"I'm sorry I asked," said Casey, rubbing her forehead. "Okay. Let's not think about that. Let's just say that it's a big black hole, and we don't have to worry about it anyway because we're going to get the rest of the pieces right. Right?"

Amun cleared his throat. "Yes, of course. Come on. Let's get two more pieces. We'll get it done twice as fast. But don't set another piece until we know these two are correct, or we'll lose track."

"Got it," said Casey. "I'm ready."

They each grabbed a building and paced around the perimeter of the map, looking for empty spaces that matched the shapes of the pieces they were holding. Casey went in first, clicking her piece into an empty square outline near the middle of the city. The rumbling started again immediately. "Not right!" Casey yelled, snatching it out of its place and searching for the next square outline she could find.

Their rule of going by twos flew out the window. What followed was a frenzy of switching places and grabbing buildings as the floor continued to rumble. Stone slabs shattered and fell down into the abyss, and a horrible crunching sound joined in from above. It was as if someone was trying to open a huge stone door, rock grinding against rock. Casey glanced up to the ceiling, and it was closing in on them—as if things weren't bad enough already.

"We better work faster, Amun! If we don't fall into the Do-what or whatever that is, we're gonna be crushed by the ceiling!"

"Don't even look at it," said Amun. "Just keep working, and watch your step!"

But Casey couldn't help looking while she worked. She wondered how they were going to get back out if they survived. The walkway was quickly falling to pieces, and the ceiling was already halfway down. The sound of crunching rock and shattering stone was so loud that it was hard to concentrate, not to mention the distraction of certain impending death. Casey kept forgetting which spots she had already tried with which buildings, but she just worked faster, frantically trying every available space.

"We're not gonna make it, Amun!" cried Casey. "We've still got four pieces left!"

"Yes, we will!" he said. "Don't stop!"

Amun hopped out of the map to run around to the other side, and a stone slab crumbled underneath his foot. His right leg slipped into the void, causing him to fall to one knee. The piece in his hand went flying, and he reached for a building at the edge of the map to keep himself from falling into the abyss. His fingers just grazed the nearest building.

Luckily, Casey was standing just inside the map and instinctively grabbed for his arms when she saw him fall. She locked onto one arm and pulled back with all her weight.

Amun regained his balance and pulled his leg out of the hole. "Thanks! That was a close one." He retrieved his building and hopped back inside the map. "Stay inside the map from now on."

They switched the four remaining pieces back and forth as fast as they could as the ceiling continued to close in on them. When it was only a few feet above their heads, Casey could barely keep a handle on the buildings she was holding because her hands were so sweaty and shaking so badly.

"Crouch down, Casey!" yelled Amun. "The ceiling is getting close! And hand me those last two pieces!"

Casey crouched down and practically threw the buildings at Amun.

He picked them up and ran, half-bent over, to the other side of the map. If she wasn't about to be crushed to death, Casey would've found that very funny. He looked like a little old man trying to win a race. When he reached the other side, he knelt down and placed the two buildings into two empty spaces near each other. Nothing happened. The ceiling kept coming.

Casey raised her hand, and it was there. "Amun!" she cried.

He switched the two buildings, and everything stopped suddenly. There was complete silence for a moment, and then the ceiling began to rise back up.

Casey and Amun came together in the middle of the map and collapsed, breathing hard and laughing nervously.

"Now *that* was close," said Casey.

"Yes, it was," said Amun. "And thank you for saving me."

"No problem. I didn't want you falling into the Do-what with evil monsters."

Amun laughed. "It's the Duat. And I didn't want to fall in there either. Not yet anyway. I'll see it when I die. It's part of the afterlife that all pharaohs go through. And it's not *all* bad, you know."

"I'll take your word for it," said Casey.

When the ceiling was back in place, all was silent. The walkway looked like a hopscotch board with a few pieces missing, and some of the stone slabs surrounding the map had fallen away too.

They hopped across two slabs toward the door in the back of the chamber.

Casey tried not to look down as she jumped from one to the other. She didn't even want to know how the stones that were left were being held up without any support beneath them. Luckily, the slabs were a decent size, probably half her body length across. It was easy to keep her balance, but it was quite unnerving to jump over a deep, black void—even for a very short distance. On the way back out, they were going to have to do it all the way down the long walkway back to the other side of the chamber. Casey didn't even want to think about that yet. She was more worried about what might be waiting for them behind door number three.

≈

Amun took the nearest torch off the wall and pushed open the door. Just as they had expected, another long passageway zigzagged down to another level. When they reached the bottom, they could hear water moving, like waves softly lapping upon a shore.

"Water?" Casey asked. "Do you hear that?"

Amun nodded and went ahead to check it out. "Looks like we're going on a boat ride."

"Are you serious?"

Casey hurried down to the entrance and found an underground river that snaked off into the distance. Torches lined each side to light the way, and right in front of them, two steps led down to a small boat that was tied to a post. There were two oars inside.

Amun held out his arm. "After you."

Casey stepped down and sat in front. Amun untied the boat and pushed off, hopping in back and taking up the oars. It was almost relaxing as they slid quietly through the water; the only sound was the soft ripple of waves underneath their boat. Along the walls, scenes depicted Ra's travels through the sky by boat.

"What do these pictures mean?" asked Casey.

"The man with the head of a falcon, sitting in the boat, is Ra," said Amun. "The yellow disc above his head represents the sun. Every morning, he gets in his boat and travels across the sky from east to west. He fights off the darkness so that we may have light, and then he travels back through the Duat from west to east every night so that he may bring the daylight once again. It also represents our life cycle: being born in the morning, traveling through our lives, and dying in the evening. See the looped cross in his hand? That's the ankh. It's the symbol for life."

"Who are the two people on either side of his boat?" Casey had always been fascinated by Egyptian mythology, and now she was experiencing it firsthand. Just a few minutes earlier, she had been a step away from meeting Ra in person during his daily trip through the Duat.

"They are the two gods that accompany Ra every day," Amun continued. "The god with the head of a bird is Thoth. See the long beak? It's an ibis. He is the god of balance and knowledge. The other one, the woman with the feather on her head, is Ma'at. She is the god of truth and justice."

Casey would have thoroughly enjoyed the boat ride if there was no fear of what might lie ahead. The paintings of the gods were so simple, yet so powerful. She could see why the Egyptians put so much faith in them. The thought of the creator, the almighty Ra, bringing the sunrise every day, accompanied by the gods of knowledge, balance, truth, and justice, made her feel safe, knowing that there were beings watching over the order of things.

She watched Ra's procession through the sky as they glided along the water, and as they reached sunset, a new god appeared. Casey had seen him before. He had the head of a jackal and was painted entirely black, except for the white kilt he wore around his waist. His head had a long snout and pointed ears that stood straight up.

"That's Anubis," Amun said. "He is the god of the dead. He protects the pharaohs and their tombs. He also passes judgment on your worthiness in the afterlife. He balances your heart on the scale. The feather of Ma'at goes on one side, and your heart goes on the other. And if he finds you're not worthy ..."

Around the very next bend in the river, their ride came to an end. Amun got out and tied up the boat, and they walked up a few steps to see what awaited them. Four entrances were guarded by statues of Anubis on either side. Each statue held two curved swords, crossed in front of its chest. The dog-headed god seemed to be looking down on the two friends menacingly, warning them not to enter.

"I think it's a labyrinth," Amun said. "And I suppose there will be consequences for going the wrong way."

"Of course," Casey groaned. "Do you have any clue which path we should take?"

Amun thought for a moment. "Well, since there are four entrances, they probably relate to the four main directions: north, south, east, and west. And since we just witnessed Ra's journey through the sky in pictures, I'm guessing either east or west would be the correct path. But I have no idea which entrance is which."

"That's okay," Casey said, perking up a little. "That's something we can work with. I've learned that a lot of times, people leave clues. Let's check the statues and the walls around the entrances to see if we can find anything."

"Good idea."

They examined the walls and the statues as closely as they could. The Anubis statues were at least seven feet tall, and it was hard to see if anything was written on their heads.

Casey tried jumping up and down to get a better look. She thought about climbing up on them, but she changed her mind when she ran her finger along one of the sword blades. It felt mighty real. Amun seemed to know what she was thinking and quickly nixed the idea, saying that it was disrespectful to Anubis and it was something she really didn't want to do.

Casey squatted down to inspect the statue's feet. It had chubby toes and even had toenails carved into them, but there was nothing else. As she grabbed Anubis' leg to pull herself up, she felt something engraved on the back of the calf. It was a small hieroglyph.

"Amun!" Casey said excitedly. "Come here. I found something. What does this say?"

"It's the symbol for north. You found it! Let's find which one is west. I think we should take west, since that's the path to the sunset, or the afterlife."

The west entrance was second from the right. They walked between the pair of statues and started down the path. The walls were narrow, eight feet high, and covered in pictures of people being struck down by Anubis' swords.

"These are cheery, aren't they?" asked Casey. "I think I like the pictures of Ra better. These are worse than the ones in the fire room."

The path zigzagged and looped and doubled back on itself. Sometimes it ended in a dead end. After turning back from several dead ends, Casey and Amun reached an intersection with two Anubis statues on either side. Amun put his arm out to stop Casey from walking through it.

"Wait," said Amun. "Don't walk past the statues yet."

Casey froze in her tracks. Amun bent down and picked up a handful of dirt. He threw it in the middle of the intersection. Nothing happened. He started looking around on the ground, but Casey already knew what he had in mind.

"Here. Try this," she said, taking the shovel out of her backpack and handing it to him.

Amun threw the shovel in the air between the two statues, and in the blink of an eye, the Anubis' came to life and sliced through the handle of the shovel with their crescent swords like it was butter. The twang of metal on metal rang through the chamber. Firelight from the torches glinted off the silver blades, making them look like sparks were flying. They moved so fast that if they had glanced away for a second, they would have missed it. Then, just as quickly, they returned to their petrified state, their well-defined bodies and limbs at the ready for the next intruder.

Casey's mouth dropped open. "Oh my God. That would've been our heads."

Amun nodded. "The question is how to get past them."

"Maybe this was the wrong path," said Casey. "If we find the right one, maybe we can just walk past."

"No. Even if we take the right path, I don't think Nekhebu is just going to let us walk by."

Casey shook her head. "If this is the right path, I'd hate to see the wrong one."

"Maybe Anubis has to judge us before we go by," Amun said.

"We're not putting our hearts on a scale!" said Casey.

"Of course not," said Amun calmly. "That's only for dead people. Watch." He took a few steps forward.

Casey grabbed his arm. "No, Amun! Stop!"

"Trust me," he said. "Anubis is a good god. He's a protector. He would not harm innocents. And I know some things from the Book of the Dead. I know just what to say."

The eyes of the statues seemed to watch Amun as he stepped between them and knelt down. The statues remained motionless.

Amun held out both arms and said, "Lord Anubis, Inpou, Anubis who is with his secrets. Lord of the secrets of the West. Lord of what is hidden. I kneel before you and bare my soul. I am an innocent. I have no wickedness in my past. My heart is clean, and my intentions are true." He looked back and waved Casey forward. "Come. Kneel next to me, and say what I just said."

Casey's heart pounded as she timidly stepped forward. She kept her eyes locked on the razor-sharp blades. Everything remained immobile, except for the eyes. Casey took Amun's hand and knelt down next to him. She repeated after him as he spoke the same incantation again, and then they stood up together.

"Ready?" asked Amun.

Even though she definitely was not ready, Casey nodded. He pulled her hand, and they walked the rest of the way through the intersection. The statues silently watched them go by.

"That was way too easy," said Casey nervously.

Amun turned to Casey and gave her a serious look. "Just remember … on the way out, we're not going to be so innocent anymore."

A shiver went through Casey's body. She seriously hoped that Miz Luna was right about all this. If she was going to steal a precious amulet from a mummy and risk being beheaded by giant black dog statues wielding swords, it had all better be worth it.

Casey and Amun cruised through the rest of the intersections without hesitation. Apparently Anubis accepted their declaration and judged them to be innocent—for now anyway. After several more wrong turns and doubling back on themselves, they finally reached the other side of the labyrinth. It led directly into King Nekhebu's burial chamber. It was similar to the one Casey had seen in the great pyramid. Just like King Khufu, Nekhebu had a great stone sarcophagus with a painted lid in the image of the pharaoh. The face on the lid was the same generic face that was painted on Khufu's sarcophagus: outlined eyes, the grand headdress of blue and gold, and the royal fake beard.

Shabti—little clay figures to aid the Pharaoh in his journey through the afterlife—were spread all around the room. Anything the king may need, they were there to provide for him. Golden jugs and jewelry and precious stones were piled in one corner. On the walls, King Nekhebu was pictured arriving in the Duat. Anubis had his heart on the scale and was allowing him entrance. Ra, Thoth, and Ma'at were standing behind Anubis, welcoming him to the afterlife.

Casey and Amun walked up to the coffin. The room was too quiet. The only sound was the crackle of the fire from the torches.

"What do we do now?" whispered Casey.

"Well, you're not going to like this, but the amulet is placed inside the mummy wrappings, over the heart of the Pharaoh, to protect him on his journey."

Casey looked at him in disbelief. "Are you kidding me? You're telling me that we have to unwrap a mummy to get it? I thought it would just be somewhere in the burial chamber."

"I told you it wouldn't be easy, but don't worry. He's dead. Help me move this lid."

This was turning into a nightmare come true, but she had survived three traps and made it to the burial chamber. There was no turning back now. Casey stood at one end of the lid, and Amun stood at the other. They counted down from three and pushed with all their might.

Stone scraped against stone, and the lid moved about an inch. They repeated the process again and again, digging their feet into the dirt and pushing, their chests heaving and sweat running down their faces from the effort. When the lid was a little more than halfway open, it tipped over the other side and fell off. Casey and Amun slumped to the ground for a few minutes to catch their breath.

"I don't want to look in there," Casey said, breathing hard.

"It's just a lot of white linen," Amun said, trying to reassure her. "And we won't touch the head. We'll just try to get through the wrappings over the chest. I really don't want to see the old buzzard's rotting face either."

Casey stood up. "Let's get this over with."

Inside the sarcophagus, King Nekhebu was wrapped up in linen that used to be white but was now a dull shade of gray. The outline of the body looked frail, and the wrappings were somewhat loose. The golden death mask on the pharaoh's face looked exactly like the face painted on the lid—except it was made of solid gold. Between that and the pile of jewelry in the room, it was no wonder there were grave robbers, and no wonder the pharaohs set up so many traps.

The death mask only distracted Casey for a brief second. There was no avoiding the unpleasant task staring her directly in the face.

"Looks like his body has shrunk," said Amun. "That's good because it'll make it easier for us to get in between the wrappings."

"Yeah," Casey said. "Hooray for us."

She reached down inside the sarcophagus and then pulled her hand back just before she touched the dead king. "I can't do it," she said. "I'm too freaked out. I've never been this close to a dead person before, let alone touching one."

"I'll hold the wrappings aside, and you grab the amulet," said Amun. "I'd prefer not to touch a thing of such great power that isn't mine, if you don't mind."

"All right. That sounds good," said Casey, feeling a bit better. She supposed she could snatch it up without even touching a thing.

Amun began to part the linen wrappings directly over where the heart would be.

Casey could tell there was something under there. It seemed to be lumpy in that area. The linen moved easily, being that it was loose, but there were dozens of layers to get through. After what seemed like an eternity, Casey finally caught a glimpse of bright blue peeking through the wrappings. Amun moved the last layer aside, and there it was, the winged scarab. The brilliant colors shined as if it were made yesterday. The blue and yellow of the wings and the orange of the sun disc sparkled in the firelight. It truly was a stunning piece of jewelry. Casey wished she could take it home with her. Modern reproductions could never do it justice.

"Go ahead. Take it," said Amun. His voice snapped her out of her trance.

"Sorry. It's just so beautiful," said Casey. "Okay, here goes nothing."

She closed her eyes, turned her head, and reached down for the amulet. Her fingers gripped the wings, and they grazed something soft and gooey underneath. She was about to let out a loud "Ewww" when she felt something else. Something grabbed her arm hard. She opened her eyes and saw the mummy's arm extended up and the hand clasped around her forearm. Casey let out a scream like she never had in her life.

Amun grabbed the dead king's arm and tried to pull it off.

"Get it off, Amun!" Casey yelled in horror. "Get it off!"

"I'm trying. He's really got a hold on you."

Casey was beginning to panic. "Break its arm! I don't care! Do anything! Just get it off!"

Amun took hold of the fingers and pulled them back as hard as he could, feeling the joints crack as he did so.

Casey wrenched her arm free, and they ran. She reached behind her head and shoved the amulet in her backpack as they exited the burial chamber and entered the labyrinth again.

"Remember, we're not innocent anymore," Amun told her. "Be ready for the Anubis statues. Run as fast as you can, and don't stop. Keep low through the intersections, and follow me."

Casey sincerely hoped he had kept track of which way to go because she had become thoroughly confused after about the third wrong turn, and if the statues were going to be slicing and dicing, she didn't want to go through any more intersections than she had to.

She ran close behind Amun, and as they approached the first intersection, he reached back and grabbed her hand. He pulled her up beside him, and just before they ran between the two statues, he yelled, "Duck and roll!" He went down headfirst into a somersault, pulling her down with him. Casey wasn't expecting to do gymnastics through the intersections, so she went down in a kind of sideways somersault that ended with her rolling one shoulder on the ground, flipping over several times, and landing on her side a few feet past the statues. As she rolled, she got glimpses of the statues above her, their razor-sharp silver blades within inches of her face.

Casey pushed herself up to her knees, disoriented, and looked around for Amun. She felt him before she could see him. He helped her up to her feet and pulled her forward again, starting to run.

"You coulda warned me about the tumbling lesson, you know," Casey said, bringing herself up to full speed.

"It was a last-minute decision," said Amun, breathing hard. "Consider yourself warned from now on because we've got a few more ahead of us. Stay next to me when we go through the intersections. We have to slide through at the same time so the statues don't have time to adjust their swings."

Through the next intersection, Casey managed a good somersault, but she lost a few strands of hair to a way-too-close sword blade. The pitch black eyes of Anubis glared at her as she dove past, and his snout grimaced, baring sharp canine teeth.

"Whoa! That was too close for comfort," she exclaimed as they cleared the intersection.

Amun poked a finger through a slit in his tunic. "Yeah, they almost got me too."

Casey was running on pure adrenaline. If she had stopped to think about it, she probably would've remained stuck in the middle of the labyrinth forever, too afraid of being diced up by the statues. As it was, she focused on running and timing her somersaults right, which was somewhat awkward with a backpack. She was in survival mode and managed to dive, somersault, and side-roll her way through the intersections without being julienned for an Anubis salad.

They finally burst out of the entrance, and Casey stopped, bending over with her hands on her knees, trying to catch her breath.

Amun looked back and yelled, "Casey, don't stop!"

She raised her head and saw one of the statues raising its sword. Amun was there in a flash, pulling Casey away and running toward the boat. Casey stumbled along beside him and practically dove into the little boat. Amun pulled the rope, pushed off, and jumped in head first.

As their momentum took them away down the river, they looked back to see all eight guardian statues with their swords raised, ready to strike. Casey and Amun looked at each other, but neither was able to say anything for several minutes as they struggled to regain their breath and their composure.

"I can't believe we just did that … and survived," Casey said when she was finally able to speak.

Amun had taken up the oars and was casually rowing back up the river. "I know. I was a bit worried there for a while."

"You know you're doomed now, right?" Casey teased. "I wouldn't want to be in your shoes when you meet Anubis in the afterlife."

"Oh, I'm not doomed," Amun said. "Don't worry about me. I never touched the amulet. That was all you. And you're lucky you're not Egyptian."

"You can say that again. I wouldn't have a chance."

They both laughed, and Casey sat back to enjoy the rest of the ride. She had never felt so grimy in her life. She was covered in sweat and dirt. She pulled the elastic out of her hair and shook out her ponytail. Dirt and sand fell to the bottom of the boat. Stealing powerful amulets from ancient mummies was dirty work. Thankfully, the rest of the way out of the tomb was uneventful. They found the map room restored to the way it had been when they first entered it. All the stone slabs were back in place, and the pile of buildings and monuments was next to the map of the city again. Then they blasted back through the wall of fire and exited the tomb into the bright, hot desert sun.

"I've got to go," said Casey as they walked back through the city. "I can't thank you enough. You risked your life for me, and I am forever grateful."

"It was the greatest adventure I've ever had," said Amun, smiling at her.

A thought occurred to Casey. What was she going to do with the amulet and the box with the key and the Moonstone? She really didn't feel comfortable burying them in the sand again. The items were just too precious, and after everything she had gone through to get them, she couldn't risk losing them. She'd be devastated. When they reached Amun's home, Casey took the items out of her backpack. She placed the amulet in the box with the key and the Moonstone and held it out in front of her.

"Amun, I have one last favor to ask," she said. "I need someplace safe to keep this box until I figure out what to do with it. Everything in here is irreplaceable. Do you have a safe place you can keep it for me until I get back? You don't even have to touch the amulet, see? It's tucked away inside this box."

Amun took the box from her. "For you, of course I will. My home is the safest place in Egypt. I will protect it for you."

Casey threw her arms around his neck. "Thank you, Amun! I'll be back as soon as I can."

She left the city and headed for the door back home, feeling much better about the safety of her box. She knew it was in good hands. Now all she had to worry about was what to do with it … and the other part of Miz Luna's message. How and where to find her might in a deep, dark cave?

Chapter 8
THE CRIMSON GATE

Casey collapsed into bed when she got home. Every part of her ached. Even her hair hurt, if that was possible. Getting up for school in the morning was going to hurt even more. Yes, there was no way she was going to be able to keep this up every night. She'd have to take a night off in between. What good would she be with no strength or energy? She was sure there were far more dangerous adventures ahead of her, and she had to be strong and alert when she went into the books.

Her alarm clock buzzed obnoxiously only minutes after she'd fallen asleep, or so it seemed. She glared at it angrily. There was no way it was already six thirty. She dragged herself out of bed and trudged down the hall to the bathroom. She had to wash off all the dried sweat before school. Her head swam with sleepiness as she stood in the shower with her eyes closed; lifting her arms to wash her hair was a great effort. She wanted to crawl back into bed so badly that she considered faking being sick, but she couldn't risk having her mom checking in on her at night. Besides, she'd have to do this who knows how many more times, and she couldn't fake being sick every time. She'd just have to grin and bear it.

After her shower, Casey went downstairs for breakfast. Her mom was already up and cooking bacon and eggs. Her stomach growled as soon as the heavy scent hit her nose.

"Morning, honey. Hungry?"

"Starving," Casey said, trying her best to sound bright and cheerful.

She felt better and more awake after she ate, but halfway through the school day, she began to struggle. Her eyes became heavy, and it was all she could do to keep them open in class. The words coming out of her teacher's mouth seemed to merge together and become nonsense. Was he speaking another language? This wasn't Spanish class, was it? She shook her head and focused on the blackboard. It was covered in equations. Nope, definitely not Spanish class. It was possibly the longest school day she had ever experienced.

When she got home after school, she went directly to her room for a nap. She immediately slipped into a deep, sound sleep.

Ryan pounding on her bedroom door startled her awake. "Casey, dinnertime! What are you doing in there? Sleeping?"

Casey sat up in alarm, looking around to see where she was. When she realized she was in her own room, she flopped back down on her pillows and yelled, "Okay! I'm coming! Geez, Ryan. Give it a rest, will ya!"

She went down for dinner and rubbed the sleep out of her eyes as she sat down at the table.

"What's up with you being all tired?" asked Ryan.

Casey's mom looked over at her as she placed plates full of spaghetti and meatballs on the table. "Are you feeling okay?" She felt Casey's forehead with the back of her hand.

Casey laughed inside to herself. That was such a Mom thing to do—and that's exactly why she couldn't fake sick. Her mom would be in her room every half hour, feeling her cheeks and forehead.

"I'm fine," said Casey. "I was up late studying last night, and they ran us in gym class today. That's all."

"Oh, well, don't stay up too late," said her mother. "You need your rest."

"I won't," said Casey. "I'm going to bed early tonight."

She could feel Ryan staring at her. Her dad had his eyes fixed across the living room at the sports channel on TV, and Samantha was trying to pretend that she wasn't texting with one hand under the table. Casey looked at Ryan, and he was staring at her with a knowing expression.

After dinner, he followed her upstairs and stopped her before she went into her room. "Come on, Case. What are you really doing? Were you studying last night? Or were you out adventuring in your books?"

"Shhh! Be quiet, Ryan," Casey scolded. "They'll hear you. And, yes, I was studying. I only go to Moonglow's on the weekends sometimes."

Ryan glared at her, apparently trying to decide if she was telling the truth or not. "I hope so. You better not be lying to me. If I find out you're letting those books take over your life again ..."

He was referring to the previous summer when she almost went to live in the jungle forever with Kamari. She had hit her breaking point with Sarah, the old school bully, and had gone into Kamari's book with the intention of staying past midnight, but Ryan had followed her and convinced her to come home. That's how he had found out about the magic of the bookshop.

"I'm not, Ryan. I swear. You know I have friends now. I have a whole life apart from the books. I'm happy. And I would never think of doing anything like that again, if that's what you're thinking."

Ryan softened again. "Okay. I was just checking, but you better keep it to the weekends. Otherwise, you'll start messing up in school, and Mom will get suspicious."

"Okay, I promise," Casey said, looking him straight in the eye. She absolutely hated lying to him, but she had to. She would not bring him into this. She refused to put him in danger.

She went into her room and shut the door. As she did her homework at her desk, her mind kept wandering off to Miz Luna's message. She'd find her might in a deep cave. What was her might? Even the rhyme talked about going to the source with all your might. Was it some sort of weapon? And if so, why was it in a deep cave? And where? A deep cave could be anywhere. She was sure there were probably dozens of books with caves in them. She pulled the chart out of her backpack and looked it over. There were so many books she'd never heard of. She had no idea if any of them involved caves, and it would take forever to read them all. Even skimming through them would take a while, and she would probably miss it anyway if it wasn't a big part of the story.

She looked at the chart again, and then it hit her. It was staring her right in the face the whole time. And she'd been there before. *Helmlock*, the medieval book she'd gone into the previous summer. The wizard lived in a deep, dark cave in the middle of a mountain. She couldn't believe she hadn't made the connection sooner. Orrick had all kinds of magical things. Maybe he had something that would help her. And what was even better was that she could keep her box there too. Orrick had a magical device that held and protected important things. She had seen it there and almost been zapped by it. He told her that it shrunk the item down and made it invisible. It protected the item with swirling rings surrounded by a force field that would knock anyone out cold who got too close to it. Yes! She was sure he'd let her use it. Orrick was very kind. And very wise. She was sure he'd know something about Miz Luna's message too.

Now she had to figure out how to get her box from Egypt to Helmlock. She'd have to take it through a series of hidden doors. She studied the connecting lines on the chart to see which books she'd have to go through. Luckily, since the hidden doors seemed to be right next to each other, she wouldn't have to travel all the way through the books and risk running into characters or getting involved in anything. She'd just pass through the doors as quickly as possible.

The chart showed three books connecting *Helmlock* and *Under the Eye of Ra*: *The Long Winter*, *Silk Road*, and *The Crimson Gate*. They didn't sound too bad, right? A little bit of snow, a very soft road, and a big red gate. No problem. She'd only be in each one for a few minutes anyway—just enough time to close one door and unlock the other.

Casey finished up her homework and went to bed early, as promised, to rest up for the next night. She was excited about her progress; she was one step closer to freeing Uncle Walt. She wondered what he might be doing in Atlantis and prayed that he was okay. She hoped he'd found his way back to Henry Mellows, and they'd survived the wrath of the gods. No matter what, he'd be there when she went back for him because once you're a character, you become just like the others. And when you read a book, if a character dies, all you have to do is start over again, and there he is, alive once more. She knew he'd be there; she just hoped nothing bad had happened to him in the meantime.

≈

Much to Casey's satisfaction, Wednesday flew by at school. It was amazing how much more fun she had and how much easier it was to pay attention when she was well rested. She laughed and joked with her friends at lunch and thought about the friends she was about to reunite with later that night. She wondered if Merewen had changed at all since their last meeting.

When she met the medieval princess, Merewen was somewhat of a rule breaker, continually frustrating her father, King Aylwin, by refusing to act like a proper lady. She was always off gallivanting in the woods, looking for adventure. She and Casey had a few adventures together, including searching out tree fairies and coming face to face with a fire-breathing dragon. It would be good to see her again, and since she was only a character in a book, Casey was guessing that she probably hadn't changed at all.

As Casey got ready to sneak out of the house that night, she realized that her shovel was gone. She had left it in Nekhebu's tomb, sliced in half by the Anubis statues. What a bummer. That little shovel had done her well. She hoped she wouldn't need it anymore since she was bringing the box to Orrick and wouldn't have to bury it any longer. She also hoped it was something that her father didn't use too often and wouldn't notice it missing. If he did, and she was asked about it, she would just deny, deny, deny. Why would she use a shovel? She would have no idea what happened to it. But, she made sure to bring along a flashlight this time. No more feeling her way along dark passageways for this adventurer.

She made sure Ryan was nowhere to be seen and left the house with her trusty yellow backpack. At least she still had that. If she were to lose that, all would be lost. There was way too much important information in there. Just thinking about losing it made her tighten her grip on the straps. She walked through the cold night and opened up the bookshop. After stepping inside and locking the door behind her, she thought of how she couldn't wait for this all to be over so she could take the dreaded paper off the windows.

Casey pulled *Under the Eye of Ra* off the shelf and let the wind overtake her. A few seconds later, she was standing under the blazing sun of ancient Egypt.

Amun was at home in the flower garden, feeding the fish in the little pond.

"No big adventures today, huh?" Casey asked, walking up behind him.

He turned around with a start. "Casey! You surprised me. You know I can't go without my partner."

"True," she said, smiling. "We've got a lot more adventures ahead of us, but they'll have to wait a little while. Right now—"

"You need your box," he finished.

"Yes. Would you mind?"

"Of course. I'll be right back." Amun scampered off and returned with the little box.

"Thank you so much," Casey said, taking the box and putting it in her backpack. "You are a great friend, and I'll be back as soon as I can, okay? Maybe we can put the amulet back when I'm done with it."

They both laughed out loud.

"I don't think I want to go through that again, but I think I can find some other things for us to get into."

"Sounds like a plan," said Casey, giving him a hug. "Don't get into too much trouble without me, okay?"

"I won't," he said. "Come back soon!"

Amun waved as Casey left the temple. She headed for the door she had come through when she left *Libertalia*. She found it next to the second hidden door, but she wasn't sure which door was which. She had been in such a rush that she hadn't paid any attention. She stared at them for a moment and then decided there was only one way to find out. She played eenie-meenie-miney-moe again, and her finger landed on the left door. She stepped up to it, unlocked it, and poked her head through. She saw thick green forest and heard a cannon blast in the distance.

"Not that one!" she said, pulling her head back and slamming the door shut. She unlocked the other door. As soon as she opened it, a blast of icy wind hit her in the face. This was definitely *The Long Winter.* She stepped into a forest blanketed with snow. She sank down to her knees in the fluffy coldness, and it immediately soaked through her jeans. *Ughh, there is nothing worse than the feeling of wet denim sticking to your skin.* The sky was gray, and the wind whipped fiercely. The wet snow stung when it hit her face.

She trudged the few steps over to the next door and heard something over the wind. It sounded like a growl and was coming from the forest off to her right. She caught something moving out of the corner of her eye, and when she turned her head, the biggest tiger she had ever seen was standing in the trees. A Siberian tiger was staring at her. He had white fur with black stripes and ice-blue eyes, and he was absolutely massive. He licked his chops and crouched down as if he were getting ready to pounce.

Casey slowly turned toward the door and raised the key to the lock, but her hand was shaking so badly that she couldn't get it in. She had to steady her arm with her other hand before she was able to slide the key into the lock. When she turned it, she heard a mighty roar behind her. She looked back to see the tiger launching himself into a full-speed run toward her. She screamed as she pulled the key out, turned the knob, and jumped through the door. She slammed it shut behind her as fast as she could, catching a glimpse of those blue eyes just before the tiger slammed against the other side of the door. The whole thing thumped from his weight being thrown against it. Thank goodness these doors were heavy, thick wood, and magical. They weren't breakable, were they? She sincerely hoped not, or she'd be in big trouble.

After taking a few long, deep breaths to calm her nerves, Casey noticed that it wasn't bitterly cold anymore. A strong wind blew, but it was a warm spring breeze, heavily perfumed with the scent of blooming plants and flowers. She was on a brick walkway; a low brick wall was on one side, and a higher wall was on the other. Mountains covered in lush greenery surrounded her in every direction. The walkway extended as far as she could see, climbing up and down the mountains.

Casey walked to the edge and looked over. The walkway was actually the top of a great wall. The Great Wall of China, to be exact. She had seen pictures of it before, but seeing it like that took her breath away, even though it wasn't the real thing. It was close enough. She should've known that the title *Silk Road* would've had something to do with China.

She had gone from Egypt to Siberia to China in a matter of minutes. These hidden doors were pretty nifty—when there wasn't a man-eating tiger waiting on the other side of them. There, on the Great Wall, she didn't see another soul. She took a few minutes to admire the view, and then she turned to the other door. One more book to get through before she reached the kingdom of Helmlock.

She opened the door to *The Crimson Gate* and stepped through. The first thing that hit her was confusion. Everything was reversed. She was standing in a meadow, looking at a forest in the distance and a river off to her left, but all the colors were wrong. The grass was blue, the sky was green, the trees in the forest were purple, and the water in the river was red. What kind of crazy book was this? The colors were so unnatural that Casey didn't like it one bit. She wasn't going to stick around to admire this one.

As she stepped toward the other door, a frantic screech reached her ears, followed by the sound of furiously flapping wings. She looked toward the woods; just inside of them, she could see a large winged creature struggling against something. She told herself to ignore it and just keep going. *Don't get caught up in anything. Don't waste any time.* The squawking and screeching and flapping continued, and her conscience wouldn't let her move on.

Casey ran over to the edge of the woods and stopped in her tracks. A bird-like creature the size of a small airplane had one of its feet stuck in a trap. It had the head and body of an eagle and a long, scaly reptilian tail. It looked at her with desperation as it continued to thrash. She stepped forward carefully and knelt down next to it. The creature hovered just off the ground, flapping its great wings and straining against the trap, which was chained to a tree.

It was almost like a shackle around the bird's leg. Casey tried to force it open without success. It was hard to keep a hold of it with the bird thrashing around, and the wind from its wings felt as if she was standing next to a helicopter. When she noticed a small button on one side of the trap, she pushed it. The trap instantly sprang open.

Before she even had time to scream, Casey was swept off her feet and lifted into the air by her backpack. She instinctively grabbed the straps and held on tightly to keep from falling. The creature had her gripped in its razor-sharp talons. There was nothing she could do. They were flying over the tops of the purple trees. If she let go and managed to survive crashing through the branches, she would lose her backpack, and that was not an option. No way. All she could do was hang on and wait for this freakishly large bird-lizard to land and hope that he wasn't planning on eating her for lunch. She must have looked extra delicious because every animal she'd run into so far seemed to want to eat her. She made a mental note to try not to look so edible next time. Maybe her bright yellow backpack looked like a giant Lemonhead. Who knew? In the meantime, Casey concentrated on controlling her fear, just as Kamari had taught her.

The bird was headed for a mountain. It began to climb higher, soaring toward a wide ledge where a nest rested in front of a cave. Casey immediately thought of Miz Luna's message. Maybe the cave she spoke of was here, and not where Orrick lived, as she had thought.

The bird released Casey just before it touched down on the ledge, and she went tumbling, coming to rest against the side of the nest. The bird settled in front of the cave and cocked its head to the side, regarding her curiously. Casey brushed herself off and stood up. The huge creature towered over her, but Casey wasn't afraid. She didn't feel any aggressiveness from it. It just sat there coolly, watching her.

Casey wasn't sure what to do. She peeked over the ledge, and it was a dizzying drop straight down for several hundred feet. There was no chance of climbing down. She turned back toward the bird-lizard. She wanted to get a look inside the cave, but he was perched right in front of it. She didn't want to risk changing his calm demeanor. Maybe he was guarding something in there.

Casey stared back at him, wondering what to do. He blinked his eyes and opened his great beak as if he was about to screech, but what came out were words. Casey staggered back a few steps in disbelief.

"What did you say?" she asked. "You can talk?"

"Of course I can talk," the bird-lizard said, his voice deep. "We can all talk here. And I said, 'Thank you for releasing me.'"

"Oh, you're welcome," said Casey.

"And I also want to know what you're doing here."

"I'm … I'm just passing through."

"Is this the truth?"

"Yes. I swear," said Casey. "I was only going to be here for a minute. I'm trying to get someplace else."

The bird-lizard blinked his eyes at her for a moment. "Well, I apologize for catching you off guard like that. I protect this land, and we are very wary of strangers. Invading forces have broken through the Crimson Gate before, and we've had to fight for our freedom. I will not let that happen again."

"I see," said Casey. "I truly meant no harm. And I'm all about freedom. So, you protect the whole land, huh? It's very … unique. I've never seen anyplace like it."

The bird-lizard stretched out one of his wings and swept it in front of him, indicating the valley below. "It's a sanctuary for magical creatures. You will find everything from sprites to leprechauns to centaurs here. Everything you've ever heard of, and even more that you haven't. We live peacefully here, but sometimes people from other places try to capture us for our magic."

"I'm so sorry," Casey said. "That's terrible."

She looked out across the valley, and the colors started to grow on her. It *was* kind of beautiful in its own weird way. She saw something moving among the trees and tracked it until it emerged onto the meadow. She inhaled quickly as a pure white unicorn stopped to graze in the blue grass. Its golden horn shone brilliantly, and it moved as gracefully as a flower swaying in the breeze. She couldn't imagine such gentle creatures being taken advantage of. It made her heart ache.

She turned back toward the creature. "What's your name?"

"I am Zephryn," he said. "And yours?"

"I'm Casey." She tilted her head toward the cave. "Are you guarding something in there?"

"Not really. I just keep things that I've … collected in there."

"Do you mind if I take a look? I'm searching for something that's supposed to be hidden in a cave. I know this doesn't make sense, but I'm not really sure what I'm looking for."

"That *is* quite strange," said Zephryn, flapping his great wings and fluttering into his nest. "But, please, in return for helping me, help yourself to whatever you wish."

Casey walked slowly into the darkness of the cave, stopping a few feet in to let her eyes adjust. When she could see what was in front of her, she found that the cave was very shallow, and items of all types were scattered across the floor. Casey started picking through them like her mother at a Saturday morning garage sale.

There were swords and shields and armor with strange symbols painted on them. There were also brightly colored cups and bowls and saucers in irregular shapes and other utensils that she couldn't identify. One neon orange gadget looked like a cross between a can opener and an electric toothbrush. She couldn't even begin to guess what it would be used for. It really was too bad that she couldn't take any of it home. Some of this stuff would've looked really cool displayed in her room, even if she didn't know what it was. She picked up one of the swords with some effort and examined it. Could this possibly be what Miz Luna meant as her might? Whatever metal it was made out of was extremely heavy. She could barely pick it up, let alone swing it to defend herself. No, it didn't seem likely that it was what she was looking for. She had a feeling that she'd know as soon as she found it—whatever *it* was.

She picked up a few of the other swords, but they were all the same. This definitely wasn't the right cave, but it did have interesting things in it. Casey was checking out some of the odd utensils when she picked up a bright red apple peeler-hairbrush-cheese grater combo. She saw a large brass pocket watch underneath it. When she opened it, there were no numbers, just a needle with four queer little symbols. The needle moved when she turned, like a compass, but instead of north, south, east, and west, it had the four symbols. At the top was a picture of the sun, at the bottom were the moon and stars, to the right was a cloud with squiggly lines beneath it, and to the left were waves.

The top and bottom were pretty self-explanatory. Sticking with the nature theme, Casey guessed that the cloud and squiggly lines stood for air while the waves stood for water. But, if this was some sort of compass, what was it supposed to lead to? How could it lead to air? It was always all around. It really made no sense. She was about to cast it aside as junk, but then she changed her mind. Maybe it would come in handy for something.

"You've got some pretty interesting things in there. Do you have any idea what this is?" she asked, holding up the pocket watch–compass.

Zephryn turned to her, blinking his sharp eagle eyes. "No, I do not. Those are all things I've collected from intruders or invaders. I have no idea what its purpose is."

"Is it all right if I take it?"

"Yes. It is yours now."

"And would you mind taking me back to the edge of the forest? I don't think I'm going to be able to climb down out of here."

"Of course. It would be my pleasure." Zephryn hopped out of his nest and crouched down next to Casey. "Please climb up on my back and hold on tight."

Casey thought she was going to have another heart-stopping flight clinging to the straps of her backpack, and she was much relieved when Zephryn told her to climb on. She put one foot on his wing and grabbed some feathers on his back to pull herself up. She scooted forward and straddled his neck, getting a firm grip on the feathers there.

"Okay. I'm ready!" she exclaimed, nervous and excited at the same time.

Zephryn flapped his great wings and lifted off. He soared down from the mountain at what felt like a hundred miles an hour before leveling off above the tops of the trees. If Casey had thought riding horses in Helmlock was a thrilling experience, this was something else altogether. It was like riding that horse at full speed times one hundred. The downward plunge made her stomach drop, and the speed was indescribable. At times, she felt as though the wind was going to tear her away, but she leaned forward, kept her head low, and held on to those feathers like there was no tomorrow. When they leveled out, she sat up straight again to watch the bizarre landscape go by.

The unicorn was still grazing in the blue grass, a gentle breeze blowing his soft white mane. Among the purple trees, a volley of little balls of light fluttered erratically, moving like butterflies, but much faster. They looked like they were playing a mid-air game of tag.

"What are those lights in the forest?" Casey shouted over the wind.

"Wood sprites," Zephryn yelled back.

Over by the red river, an elf with pointy ears gathered water in a bucket; on the other side, a creature that looked like a cross between a bear and a hippopotamus drank at the water's edge. It had the head of a hippo, but its body was covered with brown fur. It glanced up at them as they flew by.

Zephryn touched down gently near the double doors and crouched down low to the ground. Casey slid off the great bird-lizard and then hugged his feathery neck.

"Thank you for the compass," she said.

"You are welcome," said Zephryn, extending his wing and enfolding Casey in it. "We are friends now, and you are welcome here anytime."

"Thank you. I'll definitely take you up on that. This looks like a pretty interesting place to explore. As long as you don't hijack me next time. You scared me half to death."

Zephryn laughed. "I promise. I'll let you take at least five steps next time before I sweep you off your feet. But really, come back, and I will show you the rest of our home, from the Red River here in the east to the Crimson Gate that guards our land in the west."

"I will," said Casey. "Good-bye, Zephryn."

The great bird took flight. When he was soaring away high through the air, she turned to the door she had tried to go through earlier and unlocked it. She stepped through and finally stood in the medieval kingdom of Helmlock. It felt really good to be somewhere familiar. She could feel all her muscles relaxing. She thought of how funny it was that she felt so safe in a place with fire-breathing dragons, but she'd already faced one of those and survived. What else could there be?

Chapter 9
THE SWORD OF DESTINY

Casey scanned her surroundings. She had never been through this door before, but the area looked familiar. She was standing in a grove of trees and could see the spires of Merewen's castle peeking up over the tops of them. Atop the spires, the blue and gold flags of Helmlock waved in the wind. It reminded her of the first time she had entered this book. The flags were the first things she had seen, and she was ecstatic about exploring a medieval castle. She headed toward those flags and emerged from the trees on the opposite side of the castle that she was used to coming in on.

She jogged around the perimeter to the drawbridge. Everything about the castle was massive. It was as big around as a shopping mall, as tall as a skyscraper, and even the wooden double doors on the other side of the bridge were so large that it took several men to open and close them. Casey crossed the bridge, glancing down into the moat. Nope, still no alligators. It just seemed to her that a moat should be filled with alligators. You could never go wrong with a little extra protection. She'd have to mention that to King Aylwin if she saw him.

She reached the doors and lifted the heavy knocker with both hands. It slammed against the door with a great *thud*.

"Who goes there?" called a voice from the other side of the doors.

"I'm looking for Princess Merewen," Casey yelled. "I am a friend of hers. Can you please tell her that Casey is here?"

She waited ten minutes before the massive doors opened up just enough for a person to walk through, which wasn't surprising considering the size of the place. She actually found it quite impressive if they had gone all the way up to Merewen's room in the tower and gotten back in just ten minutes.

She walked through the doors into the receiving hall and saw Merewen running down the hallway with a big smile, her long, curly light brown hair bouncing up and down with each stride. She was trying to hold up her deep blue dress, but it dragged along the floor behind her. Her beagle was running beside her and barking excitedly. Guinefort jumped at Casey's feet, begging to be picked up.

"Casey! You're back!" Merewen exclaimed, giving her a big hug.

"I am!" said Casey. "It's so good to see you again!" Released from the hug, she bent down to let Guinefort jump into her arms. "And it's so good to see you too, Guiny!"

Casey laughed as Guinefort licked her face all over. "Okay, okay. That's enough. I love you too." She put the dog down and turned to Merewen.

"It's been dreadfully boring without you here," Merewen said. "No adventures. No fun at all. Father has doubled his efforts at trying to turn me into a proper princess. What do you say we go find some trouble? But no dragons this time."

Merewen smiled weakly as she uttered that last sentence, probably recalling the trauma of coming face to face with a fire-breathing dragon. Normally a brave, adventurous girl, she had completely shut down when the scaly reddish-brown creature had pursued them through the woods, burning down everything in its path. Casey had protected her and pulled her to safety until Sir Elgin came to defend them.

"Yes, we will definitely avoid those from now on, but I've actually come here with a specific purpose. I mean, besides visiting you and Guiny. I need Orrick. Can we ride out to see him?"

"Absolutely. I haven't seen him in a while myself," Merewen said. "Come, let's get to the stables before Father finds me."

Merewen had four horses that belonged to her, and this time she chose a hulking black stallion. His coat shined like dark lake water gleaming in the moonlight. Casey went for the same horse she had ridden last time, a sweet speckled gray mare with white ribbons tied throughout her mane and tail.

"Are you sure you wouldn't like a larger, stronger horse?" asked Merewen. "You are welcome to my white stallion."

"No thanks. This is my girl right here. We understand each other. Don't we, sugar?"

The mare nuzzled Casey's neck as the stable boy saddled up the horses. Then, they were off, racing through forests and across meadows toward Orrick's lair. The rocky black mountains that kept his cave secret were so high that the crests were enveloped in clouds of eerie mist.

The girls tied up their horses to a tree and began climbing around the boulders and outcroppings of the mountain, winding their way around the side to the hidden staircase that was carved into the rock. At the top of the stairs, there was an empty ledge that appeared no different from any other ledge on a mountain. But this one *was* different—if you knew the right words. And Merewen knew them.

Casey had witnessed it before, and she was no less amazed this time as Merewen placed her hands on the mountain and mumbled something under her breath. The rocks instantly disappeared, revealing an entrance to a dark tunnel.

The girls stepped through, and the rocks reappeared right behind them, leaving them in the cool dampness of the inside of the mountain. They made their way down a tunnel to the center of the mountain, and it opened up into an enormous cavern. Orrick had the most interesting home Casey had ever seen. It was filled from wall to wall with tables and cabinets full of gizmos and gadgets, pots and cauldrons, and tubes and vials containing things she was better off not knowing what they were. The thing Casey was most interested in was resting on a table not far away, its metal rings spinning softly. She spotted it immediately and then looked around for Orrick.

"Where is he?" she asked.

"I'm not sure," said Merewen. "But, there's Midnight on the couch by the oracle."

In the center of the room was the birdbath-like structure that Casey had found out was an oracle. It was filled with water and showed pictures of the future. Surrounding it were several couches and chairs, and Midnight was lounging on one of them. Orrick's black cat popped her head up at the sound of the girls' voices and lazily got up to stretch her back. She jumped down from the couch and padded her way over to the girls, purring and rubbing herself against their legs.

"Orrick!" Merewen called out. "Are you here?"

The old wizard hobbled out from the shadows on the far end of the cave. He looked frail and walked with a staff for support. He wore long dark robes and had pure white hair with a long beard. His eyes betrayed his age; they were turquoise blue and sparkled with youth and intelligence.

He clapped his hands and smiled when he saw the girls. "Merewen and Casey! How nice to see you both again! Come. Sit down. Make yourselves at home."

They all met in the center of the room and sat on the couches around the oracle.

Casey swung her backpack off her shoulders and made herself comfortable.

"What brings you young ladies here today?" asked Orrick. "Have you tired of the tree fairy necklace and want something new to play with?"

"Actually, Casey has something important to discuss with you," said Merewen. "She asked me to bring her here."

"Is that so?" asked Orrick curiously. "How can I help you, Casey?"

"Well, I have two things," said Casey, taking the little treasure box out of her backpack. "First, I was wondering if you could protect this for me. Its contents are invaluable."

"And you were thinking of the Protegus," said Orrick.

Casey nodded hopefully.

"Well, you came to the right place," he said. "Here, hand it over to me. You won't find any better protection anywhere in the world."

Casey gave him her box, and he brought it over to the machine. It made a whirring sound as its rings continued to spin, making no reaction to Orrick being so close. When Casey had gotten within a few feet, it had given her a warning not to come any closer. But apparently it knew who its master was. Orrick put the box down on the table next to it, cupped his hands around the outside of the rings, and whispered, "Secretum."

Suddenly thousands of little blue bolts of electricity covered his hands, zapping themselves into an ever-shifting electrical web. Orrick removed his hands, and the metal rings started spinning faster and faster, generating even more electricity. The web expanded out from the rings and began to form a single thick column. The little blue bolts were going crazy, zapping and connecting and moving and re-forming.

The light that glowed in the center of the machine, usually changing colors every few seconds, was now a bright fiery red. The column of electricity continued to grow until it extended out far enough to reach the box. The electric blue bolts completely encased the treasure box and lifted it off the table. The arm of electricity slowly brought it back toward the machine, but before it reached the spinning rings, the box began to spin wildly and shrink until it disappeared completely.

The electric column snapped back into the machine, the electric web blinked out, and the rings slowed down to their normal pace. The light in the center faded from fiery red back to its soft glow of ever-changing colors.

"That was fantastic," marveled Casey, stepping closer to the Protegus. It gave her a warning zap, and she backed off. "Right. Don't wanna get too close."

"No more worries, my dear," said Orrick. "It is well protected now."

With that problem settled, Casey's other question came back to her. "Speaking of protection, I was also wondering about self-protection. I mean, something to defend myself with. From what, I'm not quite sure yet, but I was told by someone that I would find my might within the deepest of caves in the darkest of mountains. Do you have any idea what that means?"

A streak of recognition swept across Orrick's face, but he remained silent. His features quickly darkened.

"You do know something, don't you?" asked Casey hesitantly. "What is it? What's wrong?"

"I'm not sure I want to tell you, my dear Casey," Orrick said softly. "It's more dangerous than you could ever imagine, and I just can't put you in that kind of danger."

"And I would never ask you to if it wasn't something of such importance that someone's life depended on it," said Casey. "Someone I love."

Orrick considered for a moment and then moved to the oracle. He stuck a bony finger in the water and swirled it around. "Come look into the oracle, my young ones. Let's see what it will show us."

Casey and Merewen stepped up to the rim of the birdbath-oracle and peered into the rippling water. As the ripples died away, a picture began to come into focus. Casey saw herself in a dark place. Blackness filled the entire scene except for a ball of blue light off to one side. She was wielding a glowing sword and wore the scarab amulet around her neck. Something moved in the darkness, and Casey began to swing her sword expertly, fighting something that couldn't be seen.

"How did you learn to swing a sword like that?" asked Merewen.

"I don't know," said Casey. "I've never swung a sword in my life. I'm pretty good, huh? I must be a natural." She laughed nervously. "I don't like the looks of that place. And what is that moving in the darkness?"

The picture dissolved, and Orrick sighed heavily. "It is as I suspected. You are meant to have the Sword of Destiny."

"That's good, isn't it?" asked Casey, looking up into Orrick's worried face. "It looks like I'm defending myself with it pretty well. Do you have it here? Tell me what's bothering you, Orrick. Please."

The lines across his forehead looked even deeper as he frowned. "That's just the thing, Casey. It's not here. It is within another deep, dark cave on the other side of these mountains. The cave is set into the cliffs that overlook the sea. Just getting there is treacherous enough."

"I'm sure I can handle it," said Casey. "I'm a good climber."

"I have no doubt of that," said Orrick. "That's not what worries me. The truly dangerous part is what lives in that cave. It is the home of the Brindyll, and he guards his treasure as fiercely as any dragon."

Merewen gasped when Orrick mentioned the Brindyll. "Oh my, Casey. You mustn't. You mustn't go there."

"What is a Brindyll?" asked Casey.

"It's a beast, covered in fur," said Merewen. "It has horns on his head and sharp claws and teeth. And it's the size of an ogre—at least ten feet tall."

"It is a solitary creature and usually feeds on the goats and sheep that roam the area around the cliffs," said Orrick. "It has killed men in the past. That's how he came to possess the Sword of Destiny. A young, inexperienced knight, seeking to prove himself, stole it from its rightful owner and went off to defeat the Brindyll and take his treasure. Needless to say, he failed. He never returned home, and the sword is now in the Brindyll's cave. It is a very powerful, magical sword, but it is useless in the wrong hands. It's not intended for everyone. It chooses its master. And it seems to have chosen to serve you next."

Casey sat back down on the couch, a little less confident than she was before. "Well, that does put a damper on things. Not only am I young and inexperienced, I don't even have a sword at all. How am I supposed to get past him? Wait till he's sleeping?"

"Certainly not," said Merewen. "That is still far too dangerous."

A light went off in Orrick's head at Casey's suggestion, and his expression changed. "Are you sure you must do this, Casey?"

"Yes," she answered. "I have no choice."

"Very well then. I have something that will help you. Waiting until he's asleep is exactly what you will do, but I strongly suggest that you take Sir Elgin with you. He is the bravest and most skilled knight we have. And after you retrieve the sword, you'll need his guidance on how to use it."

Orrick hobbled off to retrieve something from one of the hundreds of cabinets in the vast cavern. Casey stroked Midnight while Merewen sat next to her with a strange look on her face.

"Don't even think about coming with me," said Casey, guessing what Merewen was thinking. "There's no way I'm going to let you put yourself in danger."

"And there's no way I'm going to let you go alone," said Merewen. "As much as I'd like to, we can't ask Sir Elgin for help. At least, not until after we have the sword."

Casey was surprised to hear her say that. Merewen had always had a crush on Sir Elgin, and he had saved them from the dragon.

"Why can't we ask him?" Casey inquired.

"Because, silly, he would never agree to it, and he would never let us go. And the first thing he would do is go tell my father to make sure we don't try it. We'd have guards surrounding us so fast that we'd have to ask permission to use the chamber pot. And I promise I won't fall apart like I did last time."

"You're right. We can't tell anyone, but we'll have to play along for Orrick right now. And fine, you can come, but you have to promise to stay behind me. Okay, shhh ... here comes Orrick."

The old wizard returned with a little glass bottle filled with some sort of glittery gold dust. He gave it to Casey, and she inspected it curiously.

When she began to pull the cork out for a better look, Orrick said, "Don't do that just yet. You must be careful with it. And be sure not to sniff it."

"Why? What is it?" Casey pushed on the cork to make sure it was all the way in.

"It's a sleeping powder, but it is much more powerful than normal. One sniff will knock a person of your size out for a few hours. The Brindyll is much larger and will need a good dose, but you'll have to be close—and you'll have to blow it in his face."

"Oh boy. This is going to be fun. Blowing dust into the face of a beast with big sharp teeth."

"That is why you must take Sir Elgin with you," Orrick said.

"I will," said Casey, feeling badly about lying. "And thank you, Orrick. Thank you so much for your help."

The girls got up to take their leave and hug Orrick good-bye. They scratched Midnight behind her ears and started for the passageway.

Orrick stopped them and said, "Oh, and one more thing. When the time comes, don't forget to take note of the direction of the wind. You certainly don't want the dust blowing back into your own face."

"Quite right," said Merewen. "Thank you, Orrick. I'll be sure to remind her."

≈

Casey and Merewen rode their horses along the base of the black mountains until they began to smell the salty air of the sea. They wanted to approach the cave as quietly as possible. They tied up the horses to a tree and walked the last hundred yards to the bottom of the cliffs. The ocean waves crashed over the rocks and sprayed them with sea foam. Bones and skeletons of sheep and goats were scattered among the rocks and along the small sandy beach. They were slowly being dragged out to sea with each receding wave.

"Looks like we found the right place," Casey said, surveying the carnage.

Merewen tiptoed over the bottom half of a goat. "Yes. I should say we have."

A loud *thud* surprised them as a sheep carcass flew past their heads and landed in the sand next to them. Casey jumped back and Merewen let out a short scream.

"Shhh! Merewen, quiet! We have to be quiet and take him by surprise—or we'll end up like that poor sheep."

"I know. I'm so sorry," Merewen said. "It shan't happen again, although he probably already smells us."

"I'm hoping, with a little luck, that the salt air will cover our smell," Casey said. Spying a length of seaweed on the sand, a thought occurred to her. "Wait a minute, Merewen. What if we rub seaweed all over ourselves and then drape some around our necks?"

Merewen looked at it uncertainly and then picked up a piece with two fingers, holding it away from her body. "Oh my. It stinks something awful, but I think that might be a very good idea. The Brindyll will never smell us through this."

"Okay. Let's get to it then," Casey said. "Just try to breathe through your mouth."

For being a princess, Merewen certainly had some guts, Casey thought. She didn't hesitate to follow Casey to the home of the Brindyll, and now she was picking up pieces of the slimy, smelly black seaweed and rubbing it all over her pretty dress. Watching Merewen making faces of disgust and coughing quietly every few seconds was comical. Casey just hoped that Merewen wasn't going to completely freeze up and have a breakdown like she did with the dragon. Merewen had promised that it wouldn't happen again, but that remained to be seen. Still, Casey was glad to have her by her side instead of facing the beast alone.

After giving themselves a good rubdown with the seaweed and draping some around their necks, they began to scale the cliffs. The cave was about halfway up, and the climbing wasn't too bad. It was just like the climb to Orrick's cave—except there was no hidden staircase. However, there were plenty of rocks and ledges to hold on to and stand upon as they worked their way up.

They could hear the Brindyll in his cave as they climbed, grunting and growling and chewing his latest kill, crunching through the bones. Another animal carcass was flung out of the cave, flying right past the girls and almost knocking them off balance before smashing onto the rocks below. They continued to climb slowly, carefully, and quietly until the sun began to dry out their seaweed necklaces.

"Blast these wretched flies!" exclaimed Merewen softly, standing on a ledge and waving her hands frantically around her head. "And this stench! I can't take it anymore!"

Casey stopped on the ledge just above her. "I know. It's horrible," she whispered. "We're almost there. I think it's done its job; let's get rid of the necklaces."

They dropped the seaweed necklaces off the ledges, and most of the flies followed them down. Only a few remained buzzing around the girls, investigating the stink of the seaweed left behind.

"Much better," said Merewen. "Let's continue."

A few ledges later, they were standing outside of the cave of the Brindyll. They crouched against the rocks just around the corner from the entrance. The Brindyll breathed heavily and snorted. The girls looked at each other, reading each other's thoughts. They thought they had lucked out and that the Brindyll was asleep—until they felt him move, shaking the rocks they were resting upon.

Casey's heart started to beat rapidly. This creature must have been humungous to make the rocks vibrate like that. She took off her backpack and removed the bottle of sleeping powder. She popped off the cork and dumped its entire contents into her hand, closing her fist tightly around it. She'd only have one shot at this. There was no room for error. She would have to be quick and accurate. She prayed that the stuff would work instantly—or she'd be in a world of trouble.

Casey motioned to Merewen to stay where she was, but she could hear her following as soon as she started to move. Casey crept to the very edge of the entrance of the cave and peeked her head around the corner. The Brindyll had his back to them and was hunched over something fluffy and white. Even bent over, Casey could see that he was massive. The claws on his furry feet scraped the rock as he shifted his weight.

Casey took one tentative step out into the open and froze.

The Brindyll perked his head up and sniffed the air, turning slightly to the side. His sharply pointed horns curved out dangerously from above each hairy ear. He remained still for a moment and then went back to grunting and snorting over his latest snack. Casey wanted to get as close as possible before surprising him with their presence. She figured that would be her best chance of blowing the dust in his face before he had a chance to realize what was going on.

She tiptoed forward a dozen feet and then heard a rock skip across the floor behind her as Merewen tripped and accidently kicked a loose pebble. The Brindyll whipped around in fury and roared, baring his fangs and extending his arms in a menacing gesture, swiping the air with razor-sharp claws.

Merewen let out a bloodcurdling scream, and Casey gasped sharply, momentarily frozen by the ferocity of the Brindyll's roar and stature. The beast glared at them with angry red eyes, and then it lowered its head, pointing its horns at them like a bull and snorting.

Casey forced her arm to move and brought her hand up in front of her face, ready to blow.

The Brindyll charged. Casey waited as long as she dared and then shouted, "Brindyll!"

At the same time, Merewen shouted, "Casey, the wind!"

The words registered instantly. The Brindyll raised its head at the sound of its name, and Casey blew the dust right in its face. As soon as she blew the powder out of her hand, she ducked down and threw herself to the side to avoid the oncoming rush of the Brindyll.

The wind was blowing in the wrong direction, and Merewen wasn't fast enough to avoid the backlash of the powder. It all happened within seconds. The bulk of the sleeping dust hit the Brindyll square in the nose, causing him to immediately fall into unconsciousness and come to a sliding stop on the cave floor. A small amount flew back with the wind into Merewen's face, and she fainted right where she had been standing.

Casey picked herself up off the floor and ran over to Merewen, calling her name and shaking her shoulders, but she was out like a light. Luckily, so was the Brindyll. Casey looked back and forth between the two sleeping figures and weighed her options.

"Well, the Brindyll is definitely gonna be out for several hours," she said to herself. "Not sure how long Merewen will sleep. If she's out for too long, how am I gonna get her back down these cliffs? There's no way I can carry her down. No way. Man, is she gonna be mad at me when she wakes up."

Casey thought she could drag Merewen into the cave so they could hide until she woke up, but the Brindyll would surely find them if he woke up first. And there was nowhere to take her outside, except around the corner where they had first hidden, but that was no good either. That would probably be the first place the Brindyll would look. Casey decided to figure it out later. Merewen would be safe in the meantime. She had a good couple of hours before the beast would wake, and she had to get to the task at hand. The reason she had come in the first place was to find the Sword of Destiny.

She ran to her backpack and took out the flashlight. Then she ran into the mouth of the cave, leaping over the giant, hairy beast as she passed by. The front part of the cave wasn't very deep, but along the back wall, several passageways led in different directions, deep into the heart of the mountain. A feeling of déjà vu came over her as she remembered the maze in the tomb of King Nekhebu. She could only hope that these passages weren't booby-trapped, but which way should she go?

She played another game of eenie-meenie-miney-moe and chose the one in the center. She flicked on her flashlight and trotted down the passageway. The one good thing was that these passages were huge, big enough to accommodate the Brindyll, and Casey didn't feel quite so claustrophobic. There weren't any major twists or turns, and she could see a great distance in front of her. She would be able to see anything coming.

After several minutes, the passage opened up into a circular chamber with a natural pool of fresh water. Random droplets fell off the ceiling and plopped into the pool. The wall of the chamber was solid, and there were no other passages or treasures. She stepped up to the edge of the pool and looked down. She could see nothing but the shimmering greenish blue water and the rock that formed the bottom. Strike one.

Casey jogged back out and entered the next passageway. It led to what she thought was going to be a dead end, but when she approached the end of the passage, there was a large hole in the floor. She knelt at the edge and shone her flashlight down into it. She couldn't see the bottom. It was far too deep. Strike two.

"I hope he doesn't throw his treasure down there," she said aloud, listening to her voice echo. "If he does, I'm out of luck. That sword is lost forever."

She was about to leave when she saw something move in the depths of the hole. Her instinct was to get up and run, but curiosity held her there. She moved the flashlight back and forth across the emptiness, but she couldn't find anything. She chalked it up to her imagination. She pictured all kinds of ghastly creatures crawling up out of the depths. *But, really, could anything else live with the Brindyll? He probably would've killed it and eaten it for lunch long ago.*

A rushing sound reached Casey's ears. She looked back down into the hole and strained her eyes. The sound was growing louder and seemed to be coming nearer, but she still couldn't see anything. Maybe it was water? If an underground river fed the pool, why hadn't she heard it before?

A few seconds later, she saw something moving up from the depths of the hole. At first it just looked like a big black blob, but as it came nearer and the sound grew louder, Casey realized what it was. Bats. A whole colony of them. She stumbled back just in time as they rushed up out of the hole, screeching and flapping their leathery wings. They weren't concerned with Casey at all. They flew right past her, up to the top of the passageway and then followed it outside. Casey sat on the floor, clutching her chest and catching her breath, and waited for them to pass.

"Definitely no treasure down there!" she said, getting up and heading back down the passageway.

When she came out into the main area of the cave, she did a quick check of her beauty and the beast; both were still sleeping soundly. She picked one of the last two remaining passageways and tried her luck again. She hoped she wouldn't strike out a third time. She should've expected this. She had always been horrible at guessing multiple choice answers on tests at school. Even if it was a true or false question that she didn't know the answer to, she would almost always guess wrong. She always studied hard so she wouldn't have to guess.

The passageway she chose this time was longer than the others, and it had a few twists and turns. When she finally reached the end, it opened up into a vast chamber, and she knew immediately that she had hit the jackpot. The light from her flashlight bounced off a treasure trove of gold and silver, rubies and emeralds, sapphires and diamonds. It was spread all over the floor. Gold coins and rings and necklaces, silver crosses and lamps and chains, jewelry made of the most precious stones, and swords and shields all reflected their colors against the wall, making the room look like it was lit up for Christmas. Casey just stood and stared. It had to be better than any treasure ever amassed by any pirate.

After staring with her mouth hanging open for several minutes, Casey began to wade through the piles of treasure, looking for swords. She tried to remember what the Sword of Destiny had looked like in the oracle, but it just seemed to look like every other sword she had ever seen: long and sharp and silver. She picked up every sword she came across, but they all seemed too heavy for her. There was no way she would be able to swing them like she had seen herself doing in the picture—unless she somehow managed to buff up her muscles in the meantime. She could hit the gym every day after school for some powerlifting. She chuckled at the thought. Not likely.

She started digging through piles of jewelry, searching for anything hidden underneath. She found thousands of things she wished she could take home with her. If only they were real. She placed a crown on her head just for the fun of it and then tossed it aside. She wondered who the unlucky king was who lost his crown to the Brindyll. She kept moving through countless piles and then, finally, saw the hilt of a sword sticking out of one particularly huge pile toward the back of the room. Two loops curved out gracefully from each side of the handle, shining in pure silver, beckoning her to come pick it up. When she did, she almost threw it back over her head; it was light as a feather. Casey stumbled back a bit, not expecting its weightlessness. When she regained her footing, she brought the sword in front of her to examine it. A soft, silver aura began to glow around it as she held it in her hands. It felt warm and light and had incredibly beautiful detail on the hilt. Written there in the tiniest letters were the words: *Whosoever Shall Possess This Sword Shall Be Honest, Kind, And True. Only The Sword Shall Choose Its Master.* There was no question; it had to be the Sword of Destiny.

The first thing she needed to do was to find a way to carry it. There was no way it would fit in her backpack, and she'd need both arms to climb back down the cliffs. She started looking around the room, and then she remembered that one of the other swords she had found was still in its sheath with a sling attached to it. She went right to it and pulled the sword out, praying that the Sword of Destiny would fit. She inserted it into the sheath, and it slid in easily. She slung it across her back and headed out to the main part of the cave.

She collected her backpack, put the flashlight back inside, and threw it around her shoulders, letting it rest on top of the sword. Merewen! It had been over an hour since the two sleepers had been knocked out, and she had no idea how much longer the Brindyll would be down.

Casey rushed to her friend. "Merewen!" she shouted, shaking her shoulders. "Wake up!"

The princess was completely unresponsive, lying there limply with her curly brown locks spread out around her head.

Casey sat back on her knees for a minute. *What to do? What to do?* She got up and walked along the edge of the cave, scanning the cliff face on each side. There was absolutely no way of getting Merewen down while she was asleep.

As she walked back past the Brindyll, her heart skipped a beat. She thought she had seen it move. There was no way. It was too early. It was supposed to be out for several hours. Unless it just didn't inhale enough of the powder. She stopped and watched for a second, trying to hold her breath and not move a muscle.

The Brindyll snorted, pushing air out of its nose, its back rising with the intake of a deep breath, and then it was still again. Casey rushed back over to Merewen and started shaking her again. She pulled her up to a sitting position and lightly slapped her cheeks.

"Merewen! Come on. You've got to wake up!" Casey yelled. "We don't have much more time! This thing is gonna wake up soon!"

The Brindyll's body twitched as if it were trying to wake itself up, and Casey began to think desperately of what to do if it did. She now had the Sword of Destiny, which was supposedly extremely powerful. And at least it was light. She'd be able to swing it easily, but was she ready to kill something? Even if it wasn't real? Of course, she would if she had to. To protect herself and Merewen, but would she even be able to? This thing was massive. She was inexperienced and had never even swung a sword before. The beast would probably snatch it out of her hands before she even raised it over her head. *Look at the piles of treasure this thing has. Obviously many knights have tried to best him before and lost. What chance do I have?* She had to get Merewen out of there before it woke up.

Merewen stirred slightly, and it snapped Casey out of her thoughts.

"Yes, Merewen. Come on! That's it! Wake up! Wake up!" Casey said frantically as she kept an eye on the Brindyll. It continued to twitch and snort.

Merewen's eyelids fluttered and then opened halfway. She looked up at Casey and stared at her in confusion.

"Merewen, it's me, Casey. I know you're probably confused right now, and I don't have a lot of time to explain, but you were knocked out cold by Orrick's powder and so was the Brindyll. We're still here in his cave, and he's about to wake up too. I can't get you down these cliffs by myself. I need you to wake up, Merewen. Come on. Get up."

Casey stood up and pulled Merewen's arms. The princess rose on very wobbly legs, and Casey put an arm around her waist for support. Merewen squinted and looked around, trying to orient herself.

The Brindyll let out a low growl and raised its head, looking at them with half-open, angry red eyes, before dropping his head to the cave floor again.

Merewen suddenly registered what was going on and looked at Casey fearfully. "Oh my! We must get out of here!"

She started backing away from the Brindyll, and her shaky legs almost gave out from under her. Casey grabbed her again and steadied her.

"I know. We're going right now," Casey said, turning Merewen's face away from the Brindyll. "Don't pay any attention to him. Concentrate on your legs. Come on. One step at a time."

Merewen took a few tentative steps, and the beast growled a little louder behind her. She started to look back, but Casey stopped her, telling her to keep going and concentrate on walking. They reached the spot where they had climbed up, and although still somewhat wobbly, Merewen was able to hold on to the rocks as she began to climb down before Casey.

The Brindyll raised its head again and looked at Casey as she waited for Merewen to reach the first ledge. The beast let out a roar and tried to push itself up with its monstrous arms, its claws scraping against the rock, but it didn't have enough strength and collapsed on its face.

"Good job, Merewen," Casey said. "You're doing really well. I just need you to move a little faster."

Casey started climbing down quickly, a little jittery herself. The roar of the Brindyll and its scraping claws went right through her, not to mention those devilish eyes. If his strength and mobility returned before they reached the bottom, they'd be in serious trouble. Casey caught up to Merewen easily and kept encouraging her as she regained her balance and agility.

When they were about halfway down, they heard the Brindyll attempt to get up again. It must have been close to succeeding because when it flopped back down, the entire cliff face shook, sending loose rocks hurtling down to the sandy beach.

"He's gonna be up any second!" said Casey. "We've gotta kick it up another notch!"

"What in the world does that mean?" asked Merewen.

"It means climb faster!"

Soon, Merewen was back up to full speed, and they flew down the rocks from ledge to ledge as fast as they possibly could. As they neared the bottom of the cliff, a few more loose rocks tumbled past them. They looked up and saw the Brindyll peering down at them over the edge of the cave platform. It opened its mouth, baring its fangs, and let out a horrifying screech. Then, it squatted on its legs and picked up a large rock. It hurled the rock down at them, screeching and beating the floor with its fists.

"Watch out!" Casey flattened herself against the cliff face as best she could.

Merewen did the same as the rock smashed into Casey's ledge and broke off a piece of it.

Casey covered her face, protecting it from the flying debris. As soon as the rock settled, she yelled, "Go, go, go!" She was sure there would be another one following it, but they were almost down. They had to keep moving.

The pair started climbing again, and Casey looked up to see when the next rock would be coming, but the Brindyll was no longer sitting there. Instead, it had started to climb down after them with incredible speed. Casey looked back down to the ground.

Merewen was only about five feet from the bottom.

"Merewen, jump! Just jump! And run for the horses!"

Merewen glanced up, saw the Brindyll, and screamed. She let go of the rocks and fell to the ground, but she scrambled back to her feet right away and ran to untie the horses.

Casey started moving as fast as she could, and when she was a few feet off the ground, she jumped. She landed slightly off balance and rolled several times before coming to a stop. She popped up on her feet and looked up to see the Brindyll already halfway down. She started running after Merewen, but Merewen was riding toward her with Casey's horse in tow.

Casey grabbed the saddle and pulled herself up just as the Brindyll was reaching the bottom of the cliff. It turned to look at them and opened its mouth wide, letting out a ferocious roar that shook the whole valley.

Casey and Merewen dug their heels into their horses and took off at a full run, pushing the horses as fast as they would go. With their hearts pounding, they left the Brindyll behind, roaring and beating its fists on the cliff face. It broke off pieces of rock and hurled them at the fleeing girls, but they were already too far away. They could hear his roars of frustration even after they were well out of sight. When they were far enough away and felt safe, they slowed their horses down to an easy trot.

"Merewen, I'm so so sorry about the sleeping dust," said Casey. "I totally forgot to check the direction of the wind when the Brindyll charged at us."

"Not to worry," said Merewen. "I was probably more useful to you while I was knocked out than if I had been awake. As much as I love adventure and getting into trouble, it seems that I'm not very good at it."

The girls both laughed.

"I'm just glad you woke up before the Brindyll did," said Casey. "Otherwise, we probably would've ended up being a nice after-dinner snack."

"Yes, quite right," said Merewen. "What happened in there? I see you have a sword on your back. Is that it?"

"It sure is," said Casey. "I got it. And it's amazing. It's as light as a feather, and it glowed in my hands when I picked it up. You should've seen his treasure room, Merewen. Piles of gold and jewelry as tall as I am. There was even the crown of a king in there."

"Oh my. It's a wonder we made it out alive," said Merewen.

"You don't know how right you are. What should we do with the sword? Should we bring it to Orrick so he can hide it in the Protegus or should we bring it back to the castle?"

Merewen thought for a moment. "You are going to need training with it, are you not?"

Casey nodded.

"Then, I suggest we go straight to Sir Elgin. He'll be the one to train you, and he'll protect it when you're not here. We must try to avoid my father though. If he finds out what we did, he'll never let me out of the castle again."

The pair rode back to the castle and returned their horses to the stable for grooming and watering. The stable boy made a strange face at them as they left, and they couldn't figure out why until they ran into Sir Elgin. They found him alone in the courtyard where the jousting competitions were held, practicing his sword work.

"Sir Elgin!" Merewen called out as they ran across the grass.

Casey could already hear the change in Merewen's tone of voice. She was always excited to see Sir Elgin.

The knight stopped mid-swing and turned around, setting the point of his sword into the grass and leaning on the hilt, breathing heavily. He smiled and ran his fingers through his dark, wavy hair, pushing it back from his face.

"Lady Merewen and little Casey!" he said, his green eyes shining. "How very nice to see the two of you!"

The girls slowed down to a walk.

As they reached him, he took a step back and put his arm in front of his face.

"Oh my! Ladies! What have you gotten into?" he asked, speaking through his arm and sounding quite muffled. "You smell like rotten fish and seaweed!"

Merewen gasped in horror and backed away a few steps.

Casey started to laugh.

"Oh! I'm so sorry! I quite forgot!" Merewen exclaimed. "I couldn't even smell it anymore. I'm so embarrassed!"

Casey had become immune to the smell as well and had also totally forgotten about it, but she wasn't worried about offending Sir Elgin. She could see his green eyes smiling behind his arm.

"I am very sorry too, Sir Elgin," Casey said, recovering from her laughter. "We went on a little adventure and had to cover our natural scent." She reached behind her back and pulled the sword out of its sheath. The silver aura immediately began to glow around it. "We went to find this."

Sir Elgin dropped his arm from in front of his face, seeming to forget about the stench. His eyes were as wide as golf balls. "Is that what I think it is?"

Casey nodded.

"And it has chosen you for its next master?" he asked. "This is truly incredible. May I hold it?"

Casey handed it to him, and the light disappeared as soon as he touched it. He turned it over and over in wonder and read the inscription several times. He finally looked up from the sword and asked, "How did you ladies ever come upon this?"

"Well, let me tell you," Casey began, and she relayed the whole story to him.

Merewen stayed back several feet with her head down, too embarrassed to even look Sir Elgin in the eye.

When Casey finished, Sir Elgin shook his head and said, "That was incredibly dangerous! You two should never have attempted this by yourselves. It is a miracle you both survived. If King Aylwin knew about this …"

That got Merewen's attention, and she raised her head. "Oh, please, Sir Elgin. Please don't tell."

Sir Elgin calmed down and said, "Don't worry, Lady Merewen. I won't tell, but he probably will come to find out anyway since Casey and I have a lot of work to do." He then turned back to Casey. "If you must fight some evil force, little Casey, and the Sword of Destiny has chosen you as its master, then I am honored to train you. And of course I shall guard it with my life."

"Thank you, Sir Elgin!" Casey went to hug him, but she stopped short when he stepped back again.

"It is my pleasure," he said, smiling wide and laughing a bit, "but you can thank me after you've cleaned up."

Casey laughed, and Merewen gasped once more.

Casey left the sword with Sir Elgin, agreeing to start her training when she returned, and then caught up to Merewen, who was already hurrying out of the courtyard.

"I can't believe this!" Merewen exclaimed when Casey caught up to her. "I am so ashamed! What Sir Elgin must think of me now! He shall never want to come near me again!"

Casey grabbed Merewen's arm and stopped her. "Hold up, Merewen. Look at me. You're being silly. Of course he'll come near you again. He wasn't mad or offended. He just told me right now to tell you that you always look lovely no matter how you smell. Not that you've ever smelled before. And that he was just teasing us."

"Is that really so?" asked Merewen, looking hopeful.

"Absolutely," said Casey. "Don't worry about it. I've got to get home now. It's getting late, and I kind of stink."

Merewen laughed. "Yes, as do I."

The girls hugged each other good-bye, immune to each other's stench, and Casey headed off toward the door that led back home. The next time she returned to Helmlock, she would be getting trained by a great medieval knight in how to fight with a magical sword. But first, she had some research to do in the real world. And Miz Luna seemed like a great place to start.

Chapter 10
FINDING THE WAY

Casey turned off the faucet of the bathroom sink and crept back down the hall to her room. She fell into bed for another shortened sleep, making Thursday another torturously long day at school. She nodded off once during history class and then almost did a nosedive into her pudding cup at lunch. She caught herself just before the tip of her nose touched the smooth chocolate.

"You better lay off the late-night studying, Case. You need to get out more and have some fun," said Nick.

Casey gave a tired laugh and thought, *Oh, if he only knew.*

On the afternoon bus home, Casey relaxed and leaned her head against the window. She took a mental inventory of everything she had collected. Hidden safely away in Orrick's Protegus were the Moonstone, a mystery key, the scarab amulet, and an odd compass. The Sword of Destiny was in the protection of Sir Elgin. It seemed that she had found everything Miz Luna had mentioned—plus a few extras.

What to do now? Where was she supposed to go to return the Moonstone to its proper place? She figured it must be one of the books on the chart since she couldn't take the things she had collected out into the real world and would have to take them through the hidden doors. How would she find out which one to go into? And once she was there, what would she do next? She hadn't a clue.

The crisp fall air blew in through the school bus window as she thought. She took in a deep breath of the cool, smoke-tinged breeze and wondered about Miz Luna. She had to know more. The mystic must be able to give her some sort of clue as to where to go. She had communicated with the heavens before, hadn't she? And they had apparently given her clues. Why not a few more?

Casey had to find Miz Luna. And when she did, she would have to find a way to get there, which brought her to the thing she had been refusing to do since this whole thing started. She would need Ryan. He was the only one she could trust. Casey worried the rest of the way home how she would bring this up to him. But, as it turned out, he came to her.

≈

After dozing through dinner that night, Casey received another reprimand from her mother about staying up too late studying. When she excused herself from the table to head upstairs to bed, Ryan followed and slipped into her room right behind her.

"Hey! What gives, Ry?" Casey was startled to see him standing there. "I'm tired, and I need sleep."

"I know you do," said Ryan. "I can see that. Why don't *you* tell *me* what gives? And don't lie. There's no way you're this tired from studying."

Casey took one look at Ryan's face and knew she had to tell the truth, the whole truth, including asking him for help. His brows were furrowed, his jaw was set, and he meant business.

"Okay. Maybe you better sit down first."

Ryan sat in Casey's desk chair and crossed his arms.

Casey took a deep breath and started with the day she found the little black book in the bookshop. She paced back and forth across her room, stealing glances at Ryan every few minutes, trying to gauge his reaction.

He mostly stared blankly at the wall while she talked. There was no sign of anger or surprise or anything at all, which worried her more. She had hoped he would interject, ask questions, laugh, yell, or cry. Something. But when she finished, he just leaned forward and put his head in his hands, looking down at the ground.

After several minutes of silence, Casey quietly asked, "Ryan?"

Her brother raised his head and looked as tired as Casey felt. He leaned back in the chair and said, "Let me get this straight. Uncle Walt is trapped in a book, and unless you go fight some evil, magical guy with the Destiny Sword and return this Moonstone thingy, he'll be stuck there forever—and you'll eventually get stuck in a book forever too. But since you don't know where this guy is, you want me to help you find some psychic who talks to the moon. Is that about right?"

"When you say it like that, it just sounds crazy," said Casey, laughing nervously.

"Crazy is an understatement," said Ryan, getting up from the chair. He sighed deeply. "But you know I've always got your back. On Saturday, we'll go track down this Luna lady—and as much as I hate to even think about it, I'm going with you to fight this Underwood guy."

"No, Ryan! No way! Not in a million years." That was exactly what she had been trying to avoid since day one.

"Oh, yes way. And if you want my help getting to Miz Luna, you really have no choice."

Casey thought for a moment, a very long moment. She was stuck between a rock and a hard place. She opened and closed her mouth several times, ready to argue her way into convincing him not to come, but inside she knew better. She knew him too well. "Fine. Saturday it is."

≈

After a solid night's sleep, Casey was ready to spend Friday night scouring the Internet, the phone book, the newspaper—anything she could find that might lead her to Miz Luna. She struck out on every one, however. There was no mention of her name anywhere.

She found a few psychics, fortunetellers, palm readers, and tarot card diviners in the surrounding towns—and one in Oak Hill—but none of the ads mentioned Miz Luna. And it was no help that Casey didn't even know her last name.

She was stumped. Maybe Miz Luna didn't want to be found. She had literally disappeared from the festival, had she not? Casey went down the hall to Ryan's room and banged on the door, trying to be heard over his blasting music, but it was futile. She waited for the song to end. As soon as there was a moment of silence, she banged on the door again.

"Ryan! I need to talk to you!"

"Oh, sorry, squirt," said Ryan, opening the door. "What's up?"

"Geez, don't you know you're gonna go deaf listening to music like that?" Casey stepped over piles of dirty clothes on the floor.

"Okay, *Mom*. I'll try to keep it down."

Casey raised an eyebrow at the comparison and then dismissed it. "Anyway, I've been researching Miz Luna all night and can't find her anywhere. There are a few fortunetellers around, but none of them are her. And I don't know her last name or if Luna is even her real first name. What am I gonna do?"

"It seems pretty obvious to me," said Ryan. "Maybe these guys all run in the same circles. We'll go to each place to ask if they know Luna."

"Oh, yeah," said Casey, surprised at the simplicity of it and mad that she hadn't thought of it herself. "Good idea, Ry. I knew I needed you for something other than your car."

"Ha ha. Yeah. I'm not as dumb as I look. Now, get. I'm turning the tunes back up, and I'm sleeping in tomorrow. Don't bother me till noon. We'll go after lunch."

"Thanks, Ry. You're the best."

Ryan spun the volume dial, and Casey hastily exited his room. Her only hope was that someone knew who Miz Luna was and where to find her; otherwise, she'd be lost.

≈

Casey waited anxiously all Saturday morning, trying to watch cartoons or read a book, but she couldn't focus. She got dressed and put her hair up in a ponytail and then took it down. She put on a sweatshirt and then changed it for a jacket and then changed back into the sweatshirt. She just wanted to get going and wondered how Ryan could sleep in at a time like this. As soon as the clock struck twelve, she ran upstairs and pounded on Ryan's door. No answer.

"Ryan! Come on! Get up, let's go!" she yelled.

Still no answer. Then she heard a car horn coming from the driveway. She ran downstairs and out the front door.

Ryan was sitting in his old blue Mustang in the driveway.

She ran around to the passenger side and jumped in. "How the heck did you get out here? I didn't even see you come out of your room this morning."

"I've got my ways," Ryan said, grinning. "Maybe I'm magical too."

"Ha ha. Come on. Let's go."

They spent the next few hours driving from fortuneteller to fortuneteller, mystic to mystic, palm reader to palm reader with no luck. Each dark little place they entered was filled with burning incense and beaded curtains hanging from the doorways. Each lady had a "Miss" in front of her name and was dressed in long skirts and flowing blouses, but none of them knew Miz Luna.

Exasperated, Casey got back into Ryan's car and slammed the door shut. "This is not good, Ry. They all look so much like Miz Luna looked that you'd think one of them would know her. I wonder if they all go to some sort of convention where they are taught what to wear and how to make beaded curtains."

Ryan laughed. "First off, squirt, take it easy on the door. Second, don't worry. We're not done yet. Someone will know her. They have to have connections with each other. We just haven't found the right one yet."

The next one they hit was on Main Street in Maplewood, the next town over. It was nestled between the barbershop and the dollar store. The sign above the door read, "Miss Maya, Fortuneteller" and displayed in the window was a model of a Mayan pyramid with smoke rising from the top and a bare-chested god with feathered arms standing on its summit.

Casey and Ryan entered. The inside had the same Mayan theme to it; pyramids and gods were scattered here and there, and ancient Mayan stone calendars hung on the walls. In the center of the nearest calendar, a ghoulish chubby-cheeked face stuck its tongue out at Casey. She moved past it toward a young, tan, dark-haired lady at a table in the center of the room.

"Excuse me, Miss Maya? I was wondering if you could answer a question."

The lady turned her wide brown eyes to Casey. "Anything you wish, the gods will tell me."

"Well, it's not really a prophetic question. I was just wondering if you happened to know someone named Miz Luna?"

Miss Maya smiled immediately. "Why, yes, I do. She is a very good friend of mine. Why do you ask?"

"I met her at Oktoberfest. I desperately need to ask her a question, but I haven't been able to track her down. Does she have a shop somewhere?"

"No." Miss Maya shook her head. "She does private readings out of her home—mostly for people she knows or people who are referred to her. She doesn't advertise."

"Oh. It's no wonder why I couldn't find her," said Casey. "Can you tell me where she lives?"

Miss Maya studied her for a minute and then threw a glance at Ryan. "All right. The gods are telling me that your intentions are honorable. You may find her at 333 Rosedale Lane in Oak Hill."

"That's like ten minutes from my house!" exclaimed Casey. "Come on, Ryan. Let's go! Thank you, Miss Maya!"

The moon was rising as they drove down Rosedale Lane, looking for number 333. The street was sparsely populated, with no streetlights and surrounded by woods, which made it very hard to read the addresses in the dark. Casey expected to find some larger version of the tent from the festival, but it was a quaint little country cottage with a white picket fence and a rocking chair on the front porch. The kitchen light was on, and Casey could see someone moving inside.

After Ryan parked in the little gravel driveway, they ascended the porch steps and knocked on the door. A face peeked out of the window next to the front door before it was unlocked.

Miz Luna still had her long dark curly hair and bright green eyes, but her gypsy attire was missing. Instead, she wore sneakers, blue jeans, and a Minnesota Vikings sweatshirt. She recognized Casey right away. "My little friend from Oktoberfest! How ever did you find me? Come in. Come in!"

Casey and Ryan stepped through the doorway and followed Miz Luna to the kitchen. All the rooms they passed were decorated in a country farmhouse style except for one. A small sitting room stood out in stark contrast to the others. It looked like the inside of the tent at the festival. Its walls were dark with a glowing moon and stars on the ceiling and a small table in the middle surrounded by several chairs. In the bright white light of the kitchen, Miz Luna invited them to sit down at a table made of solid oak.

She ran her hands through the waves of her hair and said, "Please excuse my appearance. I wasn't expecting company. Can I offer you two something to drink? Some iced tea perhaps?"

Casey looked at Ryan for affirmation and then said, "Yes. Thank you. That would be wonderful."

Miz Luna pulled two glasses from a cabinet and reached into the fridge for a pitcher of tea.

"Are you a Vikings fan?" asked Ryan. "We're quite a ways from Minnesota. Are you from there?"

"No. I'm not from Minnesota," said Miz Luna, pouring the tea. "But, I guess I like them all right. The main reason I bought this sweatshirt is because I love purple. It's my favorite color." She laughed as she handed them the glasses.

Ryan laughed too. "Gotcha."

"Tell me what brought you here—and how you found me." Miz Luna took a seat opposite them.

"Well, my name is Casey, and this is my brother, Ryan. Lots of things have happened since I last saw you, and I really needed to ask you a question. I started looking for you on the Internet, in the phone book, everywhere, but I couldn't find you. We went around to all the fortunetellers we could find until we found one who knew you."

"Let me guess. Miss Maya?"

"Yup. That's the one."

"Well, I'm glad she told you how to find me. So, what's your question?"

"Remember the message you gave me last time?"

Miz Luna nodded.

"Well, I found the Moonstone and my protection and my might, but I have no idea where to go to return the Moonstone to its proper place. Can you help?"

"I can certainly try. Let's see what the heavens have to tell us today. Would you prefer to sit in the divining room?"

"Does it matter?" asked Casey. "Does it have to be dark, and do you have to get changed? We noticed today that all the mystics dress alike."

Miz Luna laughed her tinkling sort of laugh again. "No, my dear. It really doesn't matter. It's just that most people prefer to see us that way because that's the idea they have in their heads. They like it that way."

"I kind of like it that way too," said Casey with a grin. "Let's go into the divining room, but you don't have to get changed."

"Okay. Follow me." Miz Luna led Casey into the dark night sky room.

"I'll just wait here!" Ryan called after them, preferring to stay in the bright, warm kitchen.

Miz Luna pulled out a chair for Casey on one side of the table and then walked around to sit opposite her. Casey waited patiently as Miz Luna closed her eyes and sat perfectly still for several minutes, breathing deeply. "Okay, I'm ready." She opened her eyes and held out her hands.

Casey placed her hands on top of Miz Luna's—just as she had at the festival—and waited again.

Miz Luna closed her eyes once more and remained motionless for several more minutes. When she opened her eyes, she smiled and leaned back in her chair. Casey did the same.

"The moon and stars most certainly have a message for you," said Miz Luna.

"Really?" asked Casey excitedly. "What did they say?"

"You are to take the Moonstone into Halloween. There you will find the door that fits your key. You already have in your possession the tool that will lead the way. This must be done on Halloween night. That is when the magic of the Moonstone will be at its strongest."

Casey was quiet for a moment. She remembered seeing a book on the chart titled *All Hallows' Eve*. She didn't like the sound of it and suddenly felt nervous.

"Does that help you?" asked Miz Luna. "You look as if something's wrong."

Casey shook her head. "No. I'm all right. And yes, that helped me very, very much. Thank you, Miz Luna. I owe you big time. How can I repay you?"

"No need, my dear. It seems you have a very important job to do, and completing it will be payment enough."

"Thank you." Casey got up and gave Miz Luna a hug. "By the way, what happened to you at the festival? I went back to see you again, and you were gone. The tent and everything had just disappeared."

The mystic hugged her back and said, "Whatever are you talking about, my dear? I was there the whole time."

After collecting Ryan from the kitchen, they drove away from Miz Luna's house. Casey related the whole message to him in the car.

"Ryan, you're not gonna like this ..."

≈

From the look on Ryan's face, Casey almost thought he would change his mind about going with her, but no such luck. He was obstinate about it. He didn't like the idea of a magical bookshop in the first place. He hated the thought of going someplace that didn't actually exist—and now they would be going into a book about Halloween on Halloween night. And that book may or may not have witches, ghosts, and monsters.

Since Ryan wasn't going to back down and let her go by herself, Casey came up with an idea. A brilliant idea, if she had to say so herself. It was one week until Halloween. Throughout the week, she'd be hopping into *Hemlock* to receive sword-fighting training from Sir Elgin. On one of those nights, she would take a side trip into *Bittersweet*, buy an invisibility cupcake, and bring it through the hidden doors into *Hemlock* for Orrick to hide in the Protegus. Then, when they went into *All Hallows' Eve*, she would have Ryan eat it. It wouldn't do *her* any good to be invisible if she was going to be holding a glowing sword, but Ryan would be much safer if he couldn't be seen, right? It sounded foolproof to Casey. Brilliant. Just brilliant.

Casey slept soundly in the wake of her clever plan and woke up on Sunday morning to the scent of maple pancakes, eggs, and bacon.

As Casey wolfed hers down, her mother tuned to her and said, "I know what I wanted to ask you. While I was running around town yesterday doing errands, I happened to drive past the bookshop. I saw that the windows are all papered up. What's going on over there? We haven't heard from Uncle Walt in a while. Is everything okay?"

Casey dropped her fork on her plate. Her father looked up from his newspaper, and Ryan stared at her. His look said, *Come on. You've got to be smoother than that.*

Casey recovered quickly. "Oh, he didn't tell you? He's doing some remodeling inside. It should only be another week or so."

"Oh, really?"

"Yeah, I saw him going in there the other day with a bunch of tools," said Ryan. "Looks like he's super-busy."

"Well, I can't wait to see it when it's all done! It's about time that old shop got a facelift."

Casey and Ryan exchanged glances and promptly went back to eating breakfast.

≈

The chatter at school all throughout the next week, of course, was all about Halloween. What everyone was going to dress up as and who would get the most candy were the top topics at the lunch table. The store-bought candy bag versus the pillowcase was also a lively debate. The boys were planning a double round; they had second costumes to change into for twice the candy.

"I'm gonna be a ninja for round one and a zombie for round two," said Nick. "What about you, Richard?"

"Well, I've been told before that I bear a striking resemblance to Harry Potter. I'll be him for round one and a mad scientist for round two."

"You're not gonna carry around a plastic pumpkin to put your candy in, are you?" teased Nick.

"No! Shut up, dude!" Richard said.

"I'm just kidding," said Nick. "What about you girls?"

"Eighties Madonna," said Abby. "Complete with fingerless lace gloves and tons of hairspray."

"I'm gonna be a witch," said Miranda. "And not the good kind. The bad, ugly kind with a hooked nose and a big ol' hairy mole on my face."

Casey remained silent until they all looked in her direction, waiting for an answer. "Oh? Uh, I don't know if I'm going trick-or-treating."

"What? Why not?" asked Miranda. "Come on, you've got to come. I'm not going without you."

"What time are you guys going out?" asked Casey.

"Why? Don't tell me you've got something better to do on Halloween night than going out and getting free candy," said Nick.

"No, of course not, it's just … I don't have a costume."

"You've still got a few days left," said Nick. "You can dig something up. Meet us on Peach Street at seven."

≈

Before Casey could even consider going out trick-or-treating on Halloween, she had a plan to carry out and training to get through. The first part of her plan, to her great relief, went as smoothly as possible. She jumped into *Bittersweet* and bought a dark chocolate delight invisibility cupcake from the Le Petit Gateau Heureux bakery. She thanked Celeste and whispered to Gladys that she had found Henry Mellows and would soon be attempting to set them free. The tiny white-haired lady smiled, and a tear rolled down her cheek as Casey left the bakery.

She waved to Gladys and said, "See you soon!"

Casey then rushed through hidden doors, unlocking and hopping through them as fast as possible, not even looking at her surroundings until she made it to *Helmlock*. She had no time for tigers or pirates or anything else that might want to eat her or kidnap her. She had to get the cupcake to Orrick and begin her first session with Sir Elgin.

Merewen rode out to Orrick's cave with her, and then they met Sir Elgin in the courtyard. He was waiting for them with the Sword of Destiny in his hand and a smile on his face. "You ladies look lovely, as always. And you smell so fresh and clean!"

Merewen's cheeks flushed instantly and she curtseyed. "Thank you, Sir Elgin. Yes, that was an unfortunate happenstance—one that shall not happen again."

"And, although I'm not wearing a lovely dress like Merewen, I can assure you that I'm fresh and clean as well," said Casey. "I don't smell like rotten fish anymore. Since I don't think a dress would do for learning to swordfight, I'm wearing my lucky jeans."

"Well, you're quite right about that," said Sir Elgin. "It would be difficult to do in a dress. Shall we begin?"

Casey nodded enthusiastically, and Merewen walked off a few paces to settle herself on the grass to watch.

Elgin handed the sword to Casey and then picked up his own sword from the ground behind him. He showed her how to hold it properly and then began to show her a series of moves. She mimicked his every move as he swung from the side, dipped down low, raised the sword back up, and thrust forward on one leg. He taught her how to duck and roll and spin to avoid oncoming blows and how to read body language to anticipate her opponent's next move.

The sword glowed brightly in her hands as she learned quickly and moved fluidly; the sword's weightlessness made it easy for her to transition from one position to the next.

Merewen cheered her on as she practiced, and unbeknownst to Casey, she had another observer as well.

When Casey put down her sword to take a break, she heard clapping from the rows of seats that lined the courtyard.

King Aylwin was watching from the royal box. He came down onto the field in his royal purple robes. He was a tall, solid man with a beard and mustache and a loud, jovial voice.

He clapped Casey on the back, almost knocking her down, and said, "It looks like we've got a real knight in training here, Elgin. You better be careful—or she's likely to take your place!"

He and Elgin laughed, the king's voice booming across the courtyard.

"I don't know about my place, sir," said Elgin. "But I do think we have a knight or two that she could already outfight and outwit."

"Quite right, quite right!" said the king with a laugh.

"I do have a very good teacher," said Casey.

King Aylwin turned to Casey and said, "You and my daughter went seeking the Sword of Destiny by yourselves? Into the Brindyll's cave? And managed to retrieve it and get away with your lives? Is that so?"

Casey glanced over to where Merewen had been sitting and found that she was nowhere to be seen.

"Yes, sir," Casey said quietly.

"Well, no need to look nervous, little Casey. I'm not angry anymore, and I already gave my daughter a good talking to. I'm sure I can assume that nothing like this will ever happen again."

Casey shook her head vigorously. "No, sir."

"Good. Very well then, you should get on with your lessons. It is a great honor that the Sword of Destiny has chosen you for its master. Many of the greatest knights will never get that chance. Use it wisely. You must have a great mission ahead of you. I wish you luck."

"Thank you, sir!"

King Aylwin winked at her and strode off toward the castle.

Casey turned back to Sir Elgin. "I see Merewen skipped out on me," she said, grinning.

"Yes. I noticed she up and fled the moment she saw her father. I guess one talking to was enough for her. What do you say? Shall we hang up our hats for today and continue next time?"

Casey nodded. "Yes. I'm pooped, but it was great. Thank you, Sir Elgin. You're a great teacher, and I've learned so much already."

She handed the sword back to him, and the light died away as it left her hands.

"It's my pleasure. You learn quickly and move smoothly. You have much natural talent. We do have a spot for you here if you're ever interested!"

They both laughed, and Casey took her leave until next session.

Training was the only thing on her mind at the moment. She had only days left before she would have to fight someone—someone she assumed was going to be Furvus Underwood, a supposedly dark, evil magician—and she wanted to be as prepared as possible.

Chapter 11
ALL HALLOWS' EVE

By the end of the week, Casey was feeling pretty confident about her sword-fighting skills. Not that she was sure that would mean anything when put up against an evil magician, but she felt like she at least had a chance with the protection of the scarab amulet and the magic of the Sword of Destiny. Sir Elgin had taught her everything he could. They had crammed a lot of training into a week's time, and Sir Elgin prepared her to the best of his ability for sparring against someone who would surely be bigger and stronger than she was.

How she wished she could bring Sir Elgin with her, to have the greatest knight she knew fighting by her side. If only the characters could leave their books. They knew nothing of the real world, of not being real, and they knew nothing of other books. And that's the way it must stay. Order had to be maintained.

She was going to have Ryan with her, however, and she was starting to feel glad about it. As much as she hadn't wanted him to get involved—and as reluctant as he was about all of it—she always felt safe with him by her side. Even though *she* would have to protect *him* now—and *that* she swore to do no matter what.

Casey ran down the hall and banged on Ryan's door. The house was a bustle with ringing doorbells, passing out candy, and Samantha's blasting music as she readied herself for a Halloween party. The sun hadn't set yet, but Casey could hear her mother squealing downstairs as she opened the door for the little trick-or-treaters who came around with their parents before it got dark. Her mother gushed over each one, declaring how adorable they were and saying how much she missed having kids that age.

"Geez, what are we? Chopped liver?" Casey said to herself, standing in front of Ryan's door. "Ryan! Open up. I need something."

"What's up?" asked Ryan, opening the door. "We're not leaving yet, are we?"

"No."

"Good. I don't want to spend any more time in there than we have to."

"I know, but I need one of your old Halloween costumes."

"What for? You're not going out trick-or-treating, are you?"

"Just for a little while. We can't go in till later anyway. My friends are expecting me, and you don't want Mom to be suspicious, do you?"

"Of course not, but what are you gonna tell her about why you're out so late? She's not gonna let you stay out till midnight."

"I know. That's why we're gonna tell her that you're taking me to a Halloween party. We'll say it's at my friend's house, and you know her older brother, so you'll be there hanging out with him. That way, she'll let me go, and she won't ask to call any parents to confirm."

Ryan raised an eyebrow. "I've got to admit it. That's pretty good, squirt."

Casey buffed her fingernails on her shirt in mock pride. "I know. I know. I'm a genius."

"But why don't you let me do the talking there, genius," said Ryan sarcastically. "With the way you handled Mom's question about the bookshop the other day—dropping your fork and everything— I'll handle it. Just follow my lead."

"Fine. What about the costume?"

Ryan went into his closet and dug around for several minutes before emerging with some dark brown clothing, a hat, and a few accessories. He piled it all into Casey's arms. "Here. I was about your size when I wore this one. You're lucky I still have it. Looks like you're gonna be a pirate tonight."

Casey brought the costume back to her room and changed into the ragged brown pants, white shirt, and brown vest. She laughed to herself and thought of Tristan as she pulled on the boots and placed the hat with the feather in it on her head. How ironic that she should end up being a pirate for Halloween. Even though she knew his situation would never change since he was a character in a pirate book, she liked to imagine Tristan sailing away from Libertalia, off to pursue his dreams. She smiled at the thought and then dumped her pillow out of its case and headed downstairs.

She met Samantha in the hallway. She was dressed in a black cat unitard with two little ears on top of her head. "Don't tell me that's one of Ryan's old costumes."

"Why, yes, it is, Sam. And you can keep your snarky comments to yourself!" Casey bounded down the stairs.

Her mother was just closing the door on another round of little ghosts and goblins when she saw Casey walk into the living room.

"Oh, my little pirate! You look wonderful, honey."

"Thanks, Mom! I thought I was chopped liver by the way you were gushing over all the mini-fairies and dinosaurs at the door."

Her mother put down the bowl of candy and hugged her. "Of course not. They just remind me of you guys when you were little. And you're all growing up so fast."

"I know. I'm just kidding, Mom. Anyway, I'll be home late tonight, okay?"

"Wait a minute," said her mother, pulling back from their hug. "How late? And where are you going—and with whom?"

Before she could answer, Ryan stepped into the room and grabbed a Twix out of the candy bowl. "Don't worry, Mom. She'll be with me."

"Yeah, after we go trick-or-treating, there's a Halloween party at my friend Abby's house. Ryan knows her older brother, so he'll be there too."

Their mother raised an eyebrow. "You're going trick-or-treating, Ryan?"

Ryan snickered. "Not on your life. Casey's going with her friends, and I'll already be at the party. No costume necessary."

Their mother hesitated and glanced back and forth between the two. "I suppose that's all right. But, be careful, Casey, and be home by eleven."

"Aw, come on, Mom," said Ryan. "That's too early. Midnight, okay? Please?"

She gave them her sternest look and said, "Fine. But not a minute later."

The doorbell rang, announcing the arrival of the next wave of candy seekers and saving them from any further questioning. Their mother took the candy bowl and ran off.

Ryan grinned and bowed. "I'm good. Midnight. You can thank me later. Meet you at the bookshop at eight?"

Casey rolled her eyes and nodded. "And bring my backpack. Please."

≈

Casey met up with the gang at seven o'clock for an hour of fun before she had to get serious. She was glad for the distraction. The more she thought about what was ahead of her, the more nervous she became. She hoped the brass compass would lead her once she entered *All Hallows' Eve*. Being so busy with training all week, she had no idea what dangers lurked in the book—not to mention the danger of facing Furvus Underwood. And she had to keep Ryan safe. On top of that, she had no idea if any of this was even going to work. She thrust it to the back of her mind for an hour as she stuffed her pillowcase with as much candy as she could get.

"Okay, guys, I only have an hour because I have to go to a family party. Let's see how much damage we can do. Ready?"

Miranda looked disappointed. "Are you serious? Only an hour, and then you're gonna leave me with these weirdies?"

"You know you love us," said Nick, crossing his eyes.

"Yeah, I know. It stinks," said Casey. "I'm sorry, Miranda."

"Don't worry," said Nick. "An hour is plenty of time. These sacks will be filled by then. Then me and Harry Potter here can go get changed and go out for round two on our own."

"Go ahead," said Abby. "One pillowcase full is enough for me. *Boys.*"

The pirate, the ninja, the infamous wizard, the witch, and Madonna headed off into the night. The sidewalks were packed with trick-or-treaters. Yards were decked out with fake graveyards full of skeletons, ghosts, and tombstones. Pumpkins and candles and cottony spider webs adorned front porches.

They ran into several people from school. Sarah Templeton was dressed as a princess. No friendly greetings were exchanged as Sarah's group pushed past them. They pretended not to notice Casey and her friends at all.

As soon as they had passed each other, Casey and her friends burst into laughter.

"Some things never change," said Casey. "How lame."

A few particularly scary houses sent them running out into the street, screaming and laughing, as tall dark figures cloaked in black chased them when they tried to claim their treats.

"Oh my God," said Richard, grabbing his chest. "That guy scared the bejeezus out of me!"

"That was awesome!" exclaimed Nick, coming to a stop in the middle of the street.

"I thought that guy was fake!" said Abby. "I thought it was a statue!"

Casey stood hunched over with her hands on her knees, laughing and trying to catch her breath. "That's it for me, guys. I've gotta go, but that really was fun."

Miranda hefted up her pillowcase. "Wow. We did good. It's just about full."

"Mine too," said Casey, swinging it over her shoulder. "See you guys on Monday. Have fun!"

Nick and Richard headed off to change costumes, determined to fill two pillowcases before the night was through. Abby and Miranda went home, and Casey headed to Moonglow's.

The buzz of throngs of trick-or-treaters died away as she left the neighborhood and entered the quiet, deserted part of town. Her anxiety started creeping back in as she walked through the empty streets. She had a strong urge to turn back home and pretend that it was just a regular Halloween night. She had such fun with her friends over the last hour that she wanted nothing more than to go home and bask in it. She could sit under the bright cheery light in the kitchen and spread her loot over the table, investigating each piece. Then she could get into her PJs and watch scary movies with her family until the wee hours of the morning. Oh, how she longed to do that, rather than the task at hand, but there was no chance of it. She had to get this done, and Miz Luna said it had to be tonight. She had to think about Uncle Walter. He definitely wasn't enjoying a fun Halloween night.

She pushed all thoughts of home out of her mind and picked up her pace. She was relieved to find Ryan already waiting for her in front of the bookshop. She didn't want to have to wait around thinking about everything. She was also glad to see that he had remembered her backpack.

"I don't suppose you have a change of clothes in here, do you?" asked Ryan, swinging it off his shoulder and handing it to her.

Casey slapped her forehead. "Shoot. I didn't even think of that."

Ryan laughed. "Guess you'll be fighting the bad guy in disguise, Captain Squirt."

"Great. As if I don't look odd enough already in these books. The characters are always commenting on my strange clothes," Casey said, unlocking the door. "Come on. Let's get this thing started."

She closed the door behind them, flipped on a lamp, and flung her hat and her loaded pillowcase on one of the chairs.

Ryan watched the lumpy sack hit the backrest and settle heavily on the seat cushion. "Nice haul."

"Thanks. Wait over by the window for a minute, Ry. I've gotta get *Helmlock*."

"What's in *Helmlock*?"

"My stash," said Casey, bringing the book from its shelf. "Are you ready?"

"No, but let's do it anyway."

Casey peeled back a section of the paper from the window to let the moonlight in and placed the open book on top of the shelf in front of her. "Give me your hand."

"I really hate this," said Ryan, taking her hand in his.

She read a few words out loud. The breeze started to blow throughout the bookshop, and the light faded into complete blackness, taking the shelves and the walls and the floor beneath their feet with it. The wind picked up and blew hard around them for half a minute or so as they stood fast with their hands clasped.

It was old hat for Casey, but she knew how much Ryan disliked it. It was only his second time, but he didn't budge as the wind pelted him and the world melted away around him. His grasp was strong and steady around her fingers.

When the wind finally died and the light came back, they were standing in front of the door at the edge of the woods in sunny medieval England. Grassy rolling hills stretched out in front of them, and the spires of the castle could be seen in the distance.

Ryan let go of her hand and stepped out into the warm sun. "Wow, this is quite a difference from that jungle book I was in," he said, looking off toward the castle. "Pretty cool. What exactly are we doing here?"

"We've got to go see the wizard Orrick. He's holding a few things for me."

"Right. I do remember you saying something about that when you were laying all this on me. And how are we gonna get there?"

"I know people. And they've got horses. Follow me."

Casey retrieved the Sword of Destiny from Sir Elgin and strapped it underneath her backpack.

After a few comments from Elgin and Merewen about her strange costume, the password to Orrick's cave, and a few parting words of luck, she and Ryan rode toward the mountains. Casey could tell that he was enjoying the ride, but she held back any comments and just let him be. Maybe it would help him come around and understand the appeal of it all—why the magic of the bookshop was so special and why Casey and Uncle Walt loved it so much. The scope of what they could see and experience was limitless, and it was all waiting at the tips of their fingers. All they had to do was turn the page and read.

Casey and Ryan quickly climbed up to the cave, and Casey placed her hands on the rocky mountainside. She said, "pumpernickel."

Ryan had been quiet since they had first entered the book. He usually had a comment for everything. Casey figured he was trying to adjust to being in a magical place and didn't press him with questions.

When they entered Orrick's vast cavern, Ryan said, "Holy cow. What is all this stuff?"

"Oh, you probably don't wanna know what most of this stuff is. Orrick is a very powerful wizard. Who knows what he's got in here, but you're gonna love the Protegus. Watch this."

Orrick greeted them warmly and stepped over to the Protegus, already knowing what Casey had come for. He placed his hands around the spinning rings, said a few words, and then stepped back.

The buzzing electric arm issued forth again and produced a tiny box, which began to spin wildly until it suddenly popped to its normal size and dropped to the table.

Orrick handed the little treasure box to Casey and held her hands for a moment. "Be very careful, my young one. The danger you are about to face is greater than you know. It is malevolent, intelligent, and slippery. You must stay one step ahead. You must have eyes in the back of your head. And you must never let your guard down." He released her hands, but held her gaze.

"Thank you, Orrick. I will. Has the oracle shown you anything new?"

"No, it has not. I see you fighting against this force, but it does not show me the outcome."

"That's strange. Isn't it? Haven't you seen the victors of battles and wars in the past? King Aylwin has come to consult you before he goes into battle to see who will win."

"Yes. I have seen the outcome of many battles, but apparently yours hasn't been determined yet. That is why I am cautioning you. Please consider carefully what you are about to do."

"I have, Orrick. And I promise you that I wouldn't be doing this if there were any other way."

"Well then, Godspeed, my young Casey. May your sword aim straight and true and vanquish your enemies."

The old wizard hugged Casey, embracing her with his frail arms. It was a wonder how much power was contained in his bony fingers. He turned to Ryan and put a hand on his shoulder. "And you, young man. You protect her with your life."

"I will, sir. You can count on it."

Casey and Ryan headed back to the castle to return the horses and then made their way to the hidden doors in the woods just beyond the castle.

Casey paused before the door and took the treasure box from her backpack. She removed the compass and slipped it into her pocket.

"Why do you have a cupcake in there?" Ryan asked, leaning over so that he could see inside the box.

"I'll tell you about that later," Casey said, returning the box to her backpack. "Here's the deal. We're going to move very quickly right now through a series of doors. We have to pass through several books in order to get to *All Hallows' Eve,* and I want to get through them as fast as possible. Once we're there, I'm hoping this compass will direct us. I have no idea what to expect, but be on your guard."

"Okay. Ready when you are."

Casey unlocked the door and stepped through, turning immediately to the next one.

Ryan followed closely, closing the door behind him.

"Don't even look around, Ry. Let's just keep going."

They opened and closed, opened and closed, going through bright places, dark places, wet and snowy places. A high, shrill sound met their ears in one place, but they resisted the urge to turn around. They hurried on, pushing through door after door, ignoring anything they could see or hear as best they could.

It was hard not to turn around and investigate the strange sights and sounds that met them through each door: thick jungles, sparse deserts, heavy forests, snowy mountains, and even the edge of an ocean.

Casey knew they had arrived in *All Hallows' Eve* when they found themselves in the midst of a very dark graveyard. She held out her arm in front of Ryan. "Hold up. We're here."

Thin clouds drifted past the moon overhead. Slivers of light glinted off the old tombstones, revealing them to be broken and crumbled and covered in moss. The grass was wild and overgrown, and tangles of ivy had wound their way up the walls of the mausoleums and around the angelic sculptures. A black wrought iron gate in the distance seemed to be closing them in.

"Oh, I don't like the looks of this," said Ryan. "I hate graveyards. Especially at night."

Keeping her nerves in check, Casey said, "Don't worry. I have a sword."

"I don't think that's going to help us against ghosts or whatever we might find in here."

"But it's a magical sword." Casey was trying to make Ryan feel better, even if she didn't feel it herself. "Maybe it will work against anything."

"Guess we'll find out, huh? Which way are we going?"

Casey took the brass compass out of her pocket and opened it. The needle was pointing to the symbol for water. She turned in a circle until it pointed to the moon and stars symbol, which faced her directly at the black iron gate.

"Looks like we're going that way," she said, pointing to the gate.

"Good. Come on. Let's get out of this graveyard."

They started to pick their way around the tombstones, trying not to step directly on the graves themselves, but it was difficult because they were so close together. They moved quickly, sometimes hopping over the grassy mounds if they had to.

Casey thought she saw the ground move as she hopped over one grave in particular. She chalked it up to her imagination—or her fear trying to get the best of her—until she heard Ryan yell, "Whoa! What was that?"

Casey stopped. "What? Ryan, what is it?"

Ryan was slowly backing away from a grave. "Look! There's, like, a hand coming out of the ground. It's all bony!"

He continued to back away until something grabbed his ankle. He yelled again. Another bony hand dug itself out of the ground and wrapped its fingers around Ryan's ankle. A skeletal arm followed, and the top of a skull began to break through a few inches away.

"Kick it off and run, Ryan!" Casey yelled. "Run for the gate!"

Ryan kicked his leg and broke the hand free of the arm, the fingers still clinging to his ankle.

They ran for the gate, jumping over graves as more and more skeletal frames started digging themselves out of the dirt. Bony arms tried to grab at their legs as they flew past. Skulls and leg bones and ribcages pushed up through the grassy mounds. Full skeletons, having freed themselves, grasped onto the tombstones, trying to rise to their feet and walk.

Casey and Ryan kicked at them as they ran, shattering bones and sending skulls flying across the graveyard, but there were more emerging in front of them, near the gate, impeding their only way out. When they reached it, Casey pushed on the handle desperately, but it was no use. It was locked.

She turned to Ryan, huffing and puffing. "What do we do? There's a ton of them dragging themselves over here. We'll be over run! We can't take on that many."

"We've gotta go up and over," said Ryan, equally out of breath.

Casey looked up. "What? No way! There are spiky iron things at the top of this gate! We'll get impaled!"

"No, we won't. We can squeeze between them. And besides … we don't have much choice."

This time, Casey squealed as an arm reached out to grab her leg. The nearest skeleton had dragged itself across the ground to reach them.

Ryan kicked it off of her and then held his hands out. "Come on, Case. You've got to climb!"

She put her foot in his hands, and he pushed her up onto the gate. She climbed up a few bars and then looked back down.

Ryan was fighting off several skeletons that had reached him at the same time. They were grabbing at his legs, waist, and shirt, trying to pull him down to the ground. He had one hand gripping the gate, keeping himself from being pulled down, and with the other, he was trying to pry the bony hands off.

Casey climbed back down a few rungs and pulled out the Sword of Destiny. "Watch your hand, Ry!" She swung her glowing sword at the skeletons, easily hacking their bones to pieces and freeing Ryan.

"Thanks, squirt!" Ryan gripped the gate with both hands and began to climb.

When they reached the top, Casey slipped right through two iron spikes and began to climb down the other side.

Ryan had a bit more trouble. He was not thin enough to squeeze through, and when he tried to straddle it, he almost got hung up on his jeans. He threw one leg over, and when the other one got stuck, he jerked it hard and almost launched himself off the gate completely.

Casey gasped loudly as Ryan caught himself just in time. "Piece of cake," she said when Ryan reached the bottom.

"I knew it would be for you," he said. "I'm not quite as thin."

As they looked back through the bars into the graveyard, all the skeletons were retreating slowly back into their graves. They walked clumsily or dragged themselves across the grass to their dusty beds, scooping the dirt on top of themselves to wait for the next intruder.

"You're never gonna want to come into a book again after this, huh?" asked Casey.

"Pretty much, no," said Ryan, turning from the cemetery.

"Just remember that they're not all like this. Don't forget how awesome *Helmlock* is."

"Uh huh. So where to now?"

Casey's compass was pointing down a narrow lane that led away from the graveyard. Willows lined the small road, hanging their droopy branches over it and giving it an extra creep factor—as if the whole place wasn't creepy enough already.

"Looks like we follow the yellow brick road," said Casey.

"If only," said Ryan. "I'd take the Wicked Witch of the West over this place any day."

They followed the road as it wound through dark meadows and thick groves of trees. On their right, they passed a cornfield with a ragged old scarecrow; a large black crow on its shoulder watched them go by. On their left, they passed a quiet pumpkin patch and a rickety old house that looked like it should be condemned. There were boards across the broken windows, and the front porch was falling apart. Most of the white paint had peeled away, and the front door was hanging on by only one hinge. The house seemed to sag in the middle, giving the impression of a grim smile.

Something caught Casey's eye in one of the upstairs windows that was still intact. A blur of movement slowly crossed from one side to the other and then back again. As Casey watched the dull, gray form float by, a tingle went up her spine.

"Did you see that?" Ryan was also looking up at the window.

Casey nodded.

"Maybe this is where we're supposed to go," he continued. "Maybe the guy you're looking for is in there."

Ryan started moving toward the house, and before Casey realized it, he had one foot on the first wobbly porch step.

Casey ran forward and grabbed his arm, pulling him back.

"No, Ryan. Don't go in there."

"How do you know?"

"Because the compass is still pointing down the road. And besides, my gut tells me we need to get away from this place."

Ryan backed down from the step, and they moved back to the middle of the road. The gray form began moving faster, zipping back and forth as if it were excited or agitated. Then something popped out of the chimney, followed by another and another. One by one, dull, gray cloudy forms rose up from the chimney and began to fly circles around the top of the house. The more that emerged from the house, the faster they all flew.

The shapes of the clouds began to take on slightly human forms as they raced through the air, widening their arc around the house and expanding out toward Casey and Ryan. A chorus of low moans mixed with the rushing air, growing louder and more anguished as they came closer.

The dozens of cloudy forms mesmerized Casey and Ryan. Some of them seemed to reach out shapeless arms as they passed by.

"Okay. They definitely don't want us here," said Casey.

"I think you're right," Ryan replied. "Let's run." He took Casey's hand and sprinted off down the road.

Behind them, the moans turned to high-pitched, ear-piercing wails of agony.

Casey covered her ears and tried to look back as she ran, but Ryan stopped her. "Don't look, Casey! Just run!"

After a few more curves in the road, when they were far enough away to have lost sight of the house and could no longer hear the wailing, they slowed to a walk.

"What the heck was that all about?" asked Casey, panting.

"I'm thinking that maybe they were the former residents who were claiming their territory."

"Well, they made their warning loud and clear, didn't they?"

Ryan nodded, and they walked on in silence, keeping an eye out in every direction in anticipation of the next Halloween horror to come.

"This place makes me paranoid," said Casey, glancing over her shoulder for the hundredth time.

"I know. I'm totally on edge," said Ryan.

To their relief, they walked on without incident. When they came to a fork in the road, the compass led them to the right. They followed it straight into a small town with gas streetlamps and paper lanterns adorning old-fashioned little houses.

"Civilization!" exclaimed Ryan. "Thank goodness!"

"Yes, but I wouldn't get too comfortable," said Casey. "I wonder what year this is?"

They skirted around a town square where some boys and girls were bobbing for apples, a man played a fiddle, and the rest of the adults feasted at some sort of harvest festival. Cornstalks and pumpkins and bales of hay were scattered around the square. The women all wore long dresses, and the men wore tweed pants with suspenders. The children were running and laughing, and everyone seemed to be enjoying themselves without a care in the world. It was as if a creepy haunted house and a graveyard full of moving skeletons wasn't just up the road.

"They do look like they're having a lot of fun, and that food smells really good," said Ryan. "But I still wouldn't want to live here."

"Me neither. Our Oktoberfest at home is just as much fun, and we don't have ghosts and ghouls for neighbors."

The compass led them through the streets of the little town to the edge of a thick, dark wood. It pointed straight into the trees, but there was no path or trail to be found.

Ryan peered into the gloomy forest. "Are you sure that thing is leading us the right way?"

"I'm not sure about anything," said Casey, "but it's all I've got."

They picked their way through the dense trees, snapping branches and stumbling over roots and fallen logs. The thick canopy of leaves kept all but the thinnest slivers of moonlight from shining down into the forest, causing them to almost have to feel their way through.

Casey was about to reach into her backpack for the flashlight when an image of it on her bed flashed through her mind. She had intended to change the batteries, but she had been sidetracked by all the Halloween hullabaloo and completely forgot about it.

Branches scratched at their arms and faces. More than a few times, they walked headfirst into huge spider webs that stretched through the trees.

Casey scrambled to pull the cottony threads off her face and hair. "Hmphh! I hate this! It's not fair that I have to be first all the time. You wanna take the compass and go in front?"

Ryan laughed. "No thanks, squirt. You're doing a fine job up there."

Casey grumbled and continued to plow through the forest, trying to keep her hand out in front of her to avoid any more webs in the face.

After what seemed like an eternity, they emerged on the shore of a misty lake. A short dock stretched out into the water. Next to it, a tall cloaked figure stood at the head of a large wooden raft. The black cloak covered every part of its body. The hood hid its face, and the draping sleeves allowed only the tips of its gnarled fingers to be seen. They gripped a long wooden pole.

"Are we supposed to get on that?" asked Ryan warily.

"I think so," said Casey. "The compass is pointing straight ahead, and there's an island out in the middle of the lake."

"What if he's the grim reaper, waiting to take us to our deaths?"

"Since we aren't characters in this book, we aren't supposed to be able to die here, but the theory hasn't really ever been tested."

"Oh, great. Maybe we'll be the first."

"I really don't think he's the Grim Reaper. Why would he just be waiting here? People aren't going to come voluntarily to jump on his death ship. I think he's just a ferryman. The question is whether we have to pay him. And if so, with what?"

"Good question. Let's find out."

Casey and Ryan walked out to the end of the dock and stood next to the raft. The cloaked figure remained perfectly still, not even turning its head to acknowledge their presence.

"What should we do?" Ryan whispered.

Casey shrugged and cleared her throat. "Umm. Excuse me, sir. We'd like a ride out to that island please."

The figure said nothing and remained still.

Casey looked at Ryan, shrugged, and said, "Hello, sir? How much is a ride out to that island?"

Still the figure made no movement.

Casey threw up her hands in confusion. "I have no idea, Ry. Should we just get on and see what happens?"

"Yeah, I guess. Maybe this guy is deaf. Or maybe he doesn't have ears. I don't even want to know what's under that cloak, judging by the look of those fingers." He shuddered. "Let me get on first, though, in case he goes ballistic or something."

"Okay, but be careful!"

Casey reached behind her head and put one hand on the hilt of her sword as she watched Ryan climb onto the raft. He slowly stepped on, one leg at a time, and then lowered himself to a sitting position with his hands out in front of him. "We don't want any trouble, dude. Just a ride, if that's okay."

When nothing happened, Casey took her hand off her sword, stepped onto the raft, and sat next to Ryan. "What now?"

No sooner had the words come out of her mouth than the cloaked figure began to slowly push against the wooden pole, moving the raft out into the open water.

"That was easy," said Casey, settling in for the ride. "Ask and you shall receive."

"Yeah, almost too easy," said Ryan. "Makes me nervous."

The raft floated silently across the moonlit water, and the ferryman remained quiet. His movements were slow and smooth as he moved the pole from one side to the other. His cloak blew softly in the breeze without revealing anything underneath. Casey was glad for that; she had no desire to see what was beneath the robe.

Casey and Ryan enjoyed the silent ride in peace. Ripples across the black water smeared the reflection of the moon into a silvery puddle. They regained a sense of calm and prepared for what might come next.

When they reached the island, Casey and Ryan disembarked and said, "Thank you."

The ferryman had no response.

They walked off the dock and onto the rocky shore. They followed the compass into the trees for a short distance before coming to a door in the middle of a clearing. The only difference this door had from any of the others was that it was painted black.

Casey slipped off her backpack and rested it on the ground in front of her. "I have a feeling that we have arrived." She took the scarab amulet out of the treasure box. She produced a gold chain from her pocket that she had taken from her jewelry box at home and ran it through the beetle's wings so that she could wear it like a necklace. She strung it around her neck and then went back into the box for the cupcake.

"I need you to eat this, Ryan."

"Me? What for?"

"It'll make you invisible. And I need you to be invisible. I need to keep you safe. I don't know what we're going to face in there. And if we face a real person, I don't know for sure that we can't die."

"No way. You eat it. Don't worry about me. I want *you* to be invisible. I want *you* to be safe."

"It'll be wasted on me. My sword will still be visible, and it glows. And I'm the only one who can use it. Please eat it for me. You'll be even more helpful if no one knows you're there."

Ryan knew she was right. "Fine. Give it to me."

Casey grinned and handed him the cupcake. As he chowed down on it, she put the compass back into the box and took out the key that hadn't fit any door yet. She hoped it would be the one. She left the Moonstone in the box for safekeeping, not sure yet what she was supposed to do with it. She put on her backpack and removed the Sword of Destiny from its holster. It began to glow as soon as she touched it. "Ready?" She looked over to where Ryan had been standing and found nothing but the cool night air. "Ryan?"

"I'm here." His voice rang out of thin air. "That was a darn good cupcake, and apparently it worked. This is so weird."

"Okay, good. Follow me, and don't make a sound. No more talking, all right?"

"All right."

Casey put the mystery key into the lock of the black door and turned it. A wave of fear shot through her as she pushed the door open and stepped through. She removed the key from the lock and shoved it into her pocket as she looked around.

She was standing in a dark room. Along the far wall, there was a pedestal with a small stone bowl on top. A blue light glowed from within the bowl. The ceiling was black, but it was dotted with thousands of tiny twinkling lights. They weren't electric, but Casey wasn't sure what they were. There was nothing else in the room. Something about the walls looked funny to her. They didn't seem flat. The way the light reflected off of them made them look lumpy.

She walked over to the nearest wall and put her palm against it. She immediately pulled it back in surprise. It was rough and hard and lumpy. She looked close and felt something brush the top of her head. She ducked her head quickly and put her hand up to swat away whatever it was. She caught something and brought it down for a closer look. It was a crinkly brown leaf.

She put her sword down and took another look at the wall, putting both palms against it. She ran her hands along the bulges and found that the wall had tree branches embedded into it. There were also entire tree trunks with limbs full of dead brown leaves running throughout every wall of the room. Thick branches snaked along, sprouting twigs and leaves that reached out over Casey's head. The room seemed almost alive. Casey thought she could feel a pulse throbbing weakly beneath her fingers. But, then again, that could've been her own heart pounding.

A rustling sound tore her attention away from the wall. She grabbed her sword and whipped around to see what it was. Not sure where Ryan was—and not being able to talk to him—she thought he might have made the sound. She squinted, scanning the room from end to end, sword held tightly in her hands.

She stopped and focused on one corner where she had seen the blackness move. It was as if a piece of the darkness had torn itself apart from the rest and floated away. It moved in front of the pedestal and settled to the ground, instantly solidifying into a mass of black cloth. From beneath, a man got to his feet and brushed off his clothing. He ran his hands through his slick black hair and straightened the hem of his old-fashioned black tuxedo.

He looked straight at Casey and smiled grimly. "You've done well, girl. I never thought anyone would've made it this far. But you've had some help along the way, haven't you?"

"Underwood," said Casey, watching him closely.

"You know my name? Impressive. You've done your research. Yes, Furvus Underwood is the name. And what else do you know about me?"

"I know you're the reason that people have been forced to spend eternity in a book—even if they didn't want to. And I aim to put a stop to it."

"Well now, such strong words from such a small girl. And I see you came prepared. I really do despise hand-to-hand combat. But before we get to your silly little attempt at a coup, don't you want to know how I've done it? And why?"

Underwood's arrogance sent a blast of anger and confidence through Casey. "Doesn't much matter to me. But if you'd like a few last words and are feeling chatty, then by all means, go ahead. I'm all ears."

"I do enjoy talking about myself, so yes, I think I will." He paced back and forth protectively in front of the pedestal as he spoke, his dark eyes locked on Casey. "I'm quite the magician, you know. And my powers go far beyond pulling rabbits out of hats. I tend to lean more toward the dark side of things. Anyway, shortly after the end of the Civil War, I acquired the bookshop and discovered that it had magic in it. The person who built it was quite old and never remained in it after dark, so he never learned of its abilities.

"I reveled in them and explored everything. I went through every door I could find, and when I found this place, I knew it was something special. This room and the Moonstone are the heart of the magic. The satellite dish, as you people would say nowadays, of the power that comes from the moon and the stars. And I knew I could manipulate it. I removed the Moonstone from its pedestal and hid it along with the key to this room, thinking that no one would ever find it."

"You thought wrong about that one, didn't you?" Casey interrupted, unable to help herself. "I found your little treasure box and the chart, along with a few other things."

"Yes, yes. You're very smart." Underwood waved a hand at Casey. "Anyway, with the Moonstone hidden away, I cast a few spells of my own and *voila* … I had everlasting life inside and outside of the books, as long as each owner of the bookshop retired into a book forever, giving me their life power and sustaining me as I am. And I made sure that each owner went in, willingly or not.

"You know what the hardest part is about being alive so long? It's trying to keep other people from noticing. I had to fake my own death a few times, change my name, and go into hiding for a while. But look what good it's done now. Unfortunately, the heavens have a mind of their own and have been finding ways to help you. They hid the book and the chart from me and sent you clues. Then that blasted bird-lizard confiscated my compass. But the only way you'll ever be able to replace the Moonstone is over my dead body."

"That can be arranged," said Casey, springing forward and cutting through the air with her sword.

Underwood vanished into the blackness again, and Casey whirled around with the force of her swing. "Where are you, Underwood?" she yelled. "Too much of a coward to fight me in person? You have to hide in the dark?"

Then he was there again, standing right in front of her and holding a sword of his own.

His instantaneous appearance surprised Casey. She stumbled back a few steps, but quickly regained her footing and held her sword at the ready.

Underwood laughed, his black eyes shining. "Me afraid of you? Oh, you're a silly little girl. I just had to get my weapon."

The magician lunged, and Casey blocked him. Her sword was as bright as a star as the two blades clashed. They both drew their swords back for the next strike and began exchanging blows.

Underwood drove at her relentlessly, but Casey held her own. His size and strength made no difference against the Sword of Destiny. She was able to match each of his blows and even started to gain an advantage. She struck as hard and as fast as she could and began to drive him back.

Underwood kept inching backward, having to defend himself rather than being the one to strike. It was a position he was completely unused to, and Casey could see by the look on his face that he was becoming worried.

Casey could hardly believe it herself and kept driving forward, striking harder than ever.

Finally, Underwood's back hit the wall. He had nowhere left to go.

Casey wound up for one final blow, but Underwood disappeared. Her sword struck the wall, sending painful vibrations up her arms. She set the tip of the sword in the ground and leaned on the hilt for a moment, allowing her arms to recover. She thought that Underwood had escaped when he realized he was losing, but she heard a familiar voice scream, "No!"

She had almost completely forgotten that Ryan was there. She whirled around to find Underwood standing behind her with his sword raised over his head and a confused look on his face as he searched for the source of the voice. He suddenly slashed his sword out to the side and they heard another scream, although this time it was a scream of pain, followed by the sound of something falling to the floor.

"Ryan!" Casey yelled in terror.

Just as Underwood was turning his attention back toward Casey, she grabbed her sword and swung it as hard as she could. The blade slashed him deeply across his chest, from his heart down to the last rib on the opposite side. His black eyes were wide with surprise as he looked down and saw the gash across his body.

Just before he slumped to the ground, he pointed a finger at Casey, and a bolt of red electric light shot out of the tip.

She squeezed her eyes shut, thinking she was done for, but the amulet against her chest suddenly grew warm. She opened her eyes and saw the bolt of red light zoom across the room in the opposite direction and hit the wall. She dropped her sword and jumped over Underwood's motionless body.

"Ryan, where are you? Are you okay? You can talk to me now. Tell me where you are!" Casey searched desperately, crawling along the floor, feeling for Ryan with her hands.

"I'm here," whispered Ryan.

She moved a few feet to her left and found him on his back. She felt along his sides and pulled her hands away when one of them ran over something wet. A small pool of blood was forming by her knee. "Oh my ..." Casey put her hand over her mouth. She couldn't even get the words out.

"I know. It's not good," Ryan said softly.

"Do you think you can walk?"

"No. Not a chance."

Casey buried her face in her hands and began to cry. "I'm so sorry! This is exactly what I didn't want to happen! Oh, Ryan, I'm so so sorry! I should have never ever brought you into this."

"Case, it's okay. I would do anything to protect you. Please don't cry. It'll be okay. Just let me rest." He took her hand and held it gently.

"I wish I could see you." She knelt next to him, feeling his hand in hers.

She tore off some material from her pirate costume and pressed it against his side, holding it with one hand while continuing to hold his hand with the other. When he groaned at the pressure, she let him rest, remaining silently by his side.

Almost a half an hour later, Ryan began to become visible again. It started as a shimmering outline of his body, and it crept in, covering him from head to toe and becoming more solid as it spread. Within a minute, he was fully visible; his eyes were closed.

Casey lowered her head and watched his chest slowly rising and falling in a regular rhythm. That was a good sign. When she gently removed the cloth from his side, no more blood seeped out. Another good sign. She touched his shoulder. "Ryan, wake up."

His eyelids fluttered and then opened sleepily. "Hey, Case."

"How do you feel?"

Ryan pushed himself up to a sitting position and looked himself over.

"I feel okay," he said, surprised. He lifted his shirt where the stab wound had been and found nothing but smooth skin.

Casey threw her arms around his neck and squealed, almost knocking him over. "Yes! You're okay!" She laughed as she hugged him tight.

"Of course I am." He smiled as he regained his stability. "Did you ever have any doubt?"

"Well, yes, actually, but thank goodness for magic."

"Speaking of magic, where's Underwood?"

Casey jumped up and looked behind her.

"I killed him over there." She pointed to the spot where his body had fallen, but it was empty except for the two swords on the floor. "How can that be?"

"He must have disappeared again. Maybe just before he died. But do you think he's really dead?"

"I don't know. He was human, but he was also playing with dark magic and taking the life force from people. After I replace the Moonstone, he shouldn't be able to stay alive outside of the books. He'd be like a hundred and fifty years old or something. And the Sword of Destiny is enchanted as well, so I don't know what that did to him either. I'm not sure if he vanished and escaped or vanished and died."

"I don't think we should stick around to find out."

"You're right about that!"

Casey took the Moonstone out of her backpack and carefully placed it in the stone bowl. The pale light that had been glowing there suddenly blazed into a burst of bright blue light that lit up the entire room. It crackled as it spread across the floor and the ceiling and every wall. The twinkling lights on the ceiling started shining as brightly as stars. The dead brown leaves on the branches of the trees in the walls turned green and healthy. The sound of the pulse that Casey had thought she heard earlier grew loud and clear.

The room was alive again, pulsating with life through its walls. The brightness of the blue light from the Moonstone died down a bit, and it was like being in a forest at twilight. The stars shone above, and Casey smelled the heady scent of the leaves. She put her hands against the wall again and felt it throbbing strongly beneath. The tree trunks and branches seemed alive—not just with plant life, but truly alive.

"It's happy, Ryan. I can feel it," said Casey.

"Cool. I'm glad it's happy. I'm happy too. Come on. Let's get out of here and go home."

Casey took both swords, and they locked the door behind them, leaving the Moonstone glowing happily. They trekked back through *All Hallows' Eve* without incident.

The silent ferryman took them back across the lake, and they made their way through the forest and town. They walked swiftly past the haunted house, and when they came to the graveyard, they climbed the gate and sprinted to the door before any walking bags of bones could arise from their graves.

They continued through the doors back to Helmlock and put all the items in the care of Sir Elgin. They didn't want to ride all the way out to Orrick's again since they were anxious to get home. As they walked from the castle to the door that led back to the bookshop, they wondered what to do next.

"Should we go look for Uncle Walter to see if we can get him out?" asked Ryan.

"I'm not sure if the midnight rule is still in effect, and I don't know if we'll have enough time," said Casey. "If Atlantis is still in shambles, it may take us quite a while to find him. We might have to wait until tomorrow night."

"All right. Sounds like a plan."

"You'll come with me again?" asked Casey, turning to look at him in surprise. "I thought you would've been done forever after this adventure."

Ryan put his arm around her shoulder. "Well, it's still not my favorite thing in the world, but what do I have to be afraid of now? I've seen what you can do with a sword. And let me tell you, by the way, you were totally awesome."

Casey smiled up at him. "Thanks, Ry."

≈

When they stepped through the door into the bookshop, their problem was already solved. They weren't alone. Three figures stood over by the lamp. One of them looked quite familiar as he leaned on the counter by the cash register.

"Uncle Walter!" Casey ran over to him and hugged him tightly. "And Gladys and Henry! I'm so glad to see you all!"

"Casey! You did it," he said, hugging her back. "I knew you would. I'm so proud of you."

She stepped back and smiled up at him with tears in her eyes.

"Unscathed—and in a pirate costume no less." He laughed. "And Ryan, my boy, right by her side, I see. You two make quite a team."

"Well, Ryan didn't quite make it through unscathed," said Casey. "It was a little iffy there for a while."

"But I'm all right now," said Ryan. "Never mind me though, you should've seen Casey with a sword in her hands. This one's a regular Lancelot over here."

"Tell me how you did it," said Uncle Walt. "How did you set us free? How did you find Underwood? And how did you defeat him? Tell me everything."

"Wait a second. How did you guys know you were free?" asked Casey. "How did you know you could come out of the books?"

"There was a blindingly bright flash of blue light," said Henry. "And then something changed. It was like a weight was lifted off my shoulders that I didn't even know was there. I felt free. When your uncle said the same thing, we decided to try it."

"It was the same for me," said Gladys. "I could feel it. I just knew." The tiny lady stepped over to give Casey a hug and kiss her on the forehead. "Thank you so much."

"You're welcome," said Casey. "I still can't really believe it myself. I was so worried about leaving you in the rubble of Atlantis. What happened after I left?"

"I made my way back to Henry, and we waited out the destruction in a small back room that was well fortified. The following day, things calmed down, and then the book reset itself back to the beginning. Everything was instantly in perfect condition again, and nobody had any memory of it at all—except for me and Henry. It was really weird. And the rest of the time, we just enjoyed ourselves and waited to see what would happen."

"Man, and all that time I was worried that you were smashed to pieces or stuck at the bottom of the ocean somewhere. And there you were relaxing and enjoying yourself," Casey teased. "And we've got to find you some more modern clothing, Henry. After tonight, I don't think you'll want to be walking around in a toga."

Everyone laughed.

Henry looked down at himself and said, "You're quite right about that."

"I think I can dig something out of my closet for you," said Uncle Walt. "Casey, where's the black book? Let's have a look at it."

Casey pulled it out of her backpack and opened it for everyone to see. As they flipped through the pages, they found that it had changed. Both rhymes were gone, and the end of the chapters for Gladys and Henry no longer said that they had retired into their respective books. The last sentence for each of them now said: *Given new life.* There was not a word about Underwood anywhere in the book.

Casey smiled and walked over to the window. She tore down a piece of the construction paper and gazed up at the moon. "Thank you," she whispered. Then she realized that someone was missing. "Hey, what about Mr. Appleby? Where is he?"

"Oh, you know Tom," said Uncle Walt. "My guess is that he has no desire to return to the real world. He's happy as a clam in the Old West. We'll have to make a trip out there to tell him what happened. By the way, why are all the windows covered in construction paper?"

Casey laughed. "Well, I didn't know how long this was gonna take, so I put up a sign that said you were closed for remodeling."

"Good idea, but what am I gonna tell people when they see that nothing has been remodeled? I can't change this place. It's a classic. I love it the way it is."

"That's true," said Casey. "I didn't think of that. And my mom has already asked me about it."

Ryan looked around the place, scratched his head, and said, "Just buy a new lamp. How about that?"

Everyone laughed, and Uncle Walt said, "Perfect. I'll hit the mall this week." He moved to a chair and motioned for everyone else to sit too. "Now tell me everything."

≈

Casey had to wait an entire week to jump back into a book again, and it couldn't come soon enough. Everything was back to normal, and she had a full week of school and homework to get through before she could get to the one place she had been dying to go for ages. It seemed like forever since she had been into the jungle to visit Kamari. She was bursting at the seams to tell him everything that had happened, but she would have to change a few things since he was a character in a book. She could never let him find out otherwise. Aside from that, no one listened to her like Kamari did. She could tell him anything, and he always had the perfect advice. Since she went to visit him the most, she wondered what would happen as she continued to grow while he would always remain the same. Would he notice? Would he begin to ask questions? And if he did, what would she say?

There was still some time before those things would arise—if they ever did. For now, Casey was as happy as could be. She rushed to the bookshop the following Friday night as soon as she could get away.

As usual, Kamari was sharpening arrows outside his hut. He jumped up with delight when he saw her coming. "Suhuba! It has been so long! Come sit and tell me how you've been. I've missed you!"

"I've missed you terribly too," Casey said as she sat down next to him. "And, boy, do I have a story to tell you! Listen to this …"

Made in the USA
San Bernardino, CA
15 June 2014